AFTER DACHAU

BOOKS BY DANIEL QUINN

Ishmael

The Story of B

Providence:
The Story of a Fifty-Year Vision Quest

My Ishmael: A Sequel

Beyond Civilization:
Humanity's Next Great Adventure

A NOVEL

AFTER DACHAU

DANIEL QUINN

CONTEXT BOOKS
NEW YORK

All rights reserved under International and
Pan-American Copyright Conventions.
Published in the United States of America
by Context Books, New York.

www.contextbooks.com

Designer: Cassandra J. Pappas
Jacket design: Archie Ferguson
Typeface: Monotype Sabon

Context Books
368 Broadway
Suite 314
New York, NY 10013

Library of Congress Cataloging-in-Publication Data

Quinn, Daniel.
  After Dachau : a novel / Daniel Quinn.
    p. cm.
  ISBN 1-893956-13-X (alk. paper)
  1. Children of the rich—Fiction. 2. Reincarnation—
Fiction. 3. Young men—Fiction. I. Title.
  PS3567.U338 A69 2001
  813'.54—dc21

                                      00-012191

  9 8 7 6 5 4 3 2
Manufactured in the United States of America

For Beau Friedlander,
prince of publishers

The epigraphs introducing the various sections of this book are all from *Vampires, Burial, and Death: Folklore and Reality,* by Paul Barber.

PART ONE

FORGOTTEN

Bodies do not always stay buried.

1

ALL CHILDREN OF the rich and famous grow up believing they were switched at birth for the infants their parents *really* wanted, and I'm no exception. I'm Jason Tull—but not the rich and famous one, obviously. That's my father.

Had my parents been given the infant they wanted, he would have grown up behaving exactly like a rightful heir, which is a thing I understand perfectly well but have never been able to do (and have rarely seen anyone else do). Perhaps it's something genetic. Rightful heirs have special genes that kick in and take over at age five or six, and the rest of us don't.

Naturally Mom and Dad assured me that nothing at all was expected of me just because I happened to be their son. They loved me for myself, and so on. But as one nears the end of school life (in my case, in the year 1992), the people close to you begin to hold their breath—to see if you're possibly going to begin acting like a rightful heir after all. I didn't, and before long everyone began to breathe normally again.

Instead of behaving like the rightful heir, I conceived an eccentric interest. This was the way my relatives perceived it, not the way I perceived it. Having nothing else in particular to live for, I found a hobby (they must have thought)—and a bizarre one to boot, just to prove I'm special. It irked me that they thought this way about it, but I know I might think the same in their place.

In my sophomore year at prep school I spent spring vacation with another son of rich and famous parents. My friend's mother was a gaunt and melancholy person who whiled away her days reading. Mornings she spent in the morning room. After lunch she moved to one of several rooms that counted as living rooms. When the sun began its decline, she donned a sweater and moved to a shady spot by the pool. In the evening, before taking her book to bed, she seemed to feel obliged to spend an hour or two with the young master and his friend—a period that was painful to get through, as she was so clearly bored to stupefaction by the two of us.

All this leads up to the fact that I took a fancy to one of her books, which she'd left unguarded for a moment on the arm of a chair. I only had time to read the dust-jacket notes, which heightened my interest, and I began to wonder how I could get hold of it when she was done. She was the sort of person who would think it an impertinence to suggest that I might read the same books as she. A sort of sumptuary thing, like only kings wearing purple. She somehow gave the impression that the books she read had been written on commission for her exclusive use.

It was an impertinence even to ask what I actually asked, which was (in a very offhand way), "What do you *do* with all the books you read? Do you keep them somewhere here or donate them to a library or what?"

She was instantly on her guard—against what, I can't guess.

She explained that her maid took them to a used-book dealer who evidently had the royal entitlement to resell all her paper castoffs. The rich mostly know very well how to pinch a penny.

The next day I angled in on the maid. You never know. Some servants are even haughtier than the people they serve, but I was lucky with this one, and a few hours later the book was delivered into my hands. It didn't occur to me at the time that this book (or any book) was going to shape the direction of my life. At this age I didn't even know that lives can *have* a direction.

2

IT WAS A STORY—purportedly a true story—about something that happened in a small midwestern town in the middle of the nineteenth century. I suppose it's silly of me to be cagey about this. I later learned that this case was well known to people interested in such things, but at the time I not only didn't know it was a well-known case, I didn't even know it was a case—meaning an instance of a phenomenon. I thought I was reading about an event unparalleled in human history, completely unique.

In Vettsburg, Missouri, a little girl by the name of Mary Anne Dorson surprised her mother one day by starting to gossip about some people who lived on the other side of town, the Prescotts. The reason this surprised Mrs. Dorson was that the Dorsons didn't know the Prescotts, though they were vaguely aware of their existence. She asked Mary Anne if she had met the Prescott children at school, and the little girl explained that the Prescott children were much grown up, no longer in school, though still living at home. So how did Mary Anne know them?

"I guess I know them from my dreams," Mary Anne said.

This didn't please her mother, who liked to think she was bringing up a child with her feet planted on the ground. She didn't pursue the subject, but this didn't end it either. Mary Anne not only went on talking, she began bringing forth details she couldn't possibly know by any means whatever, which could only suggest she was making them up, fabricating them—lying, in short. Mrs. Dorson told her daughter very firmly that she didn't intend to hear any more of this nonsense, not another word of it.

Stunned, Mary Anne fell silent. It was the beginning of summer in her eighth year. By the middle of the summer, the entire family was engulfed in her silence, which oppressed them like the still air before a thunderstorm. Mary Anne's dresses hung on her like rags. She was losing weight, melting before their eyes. They took her to the family doctor, Dr. Jansen (telling him nothing of the Prescott business, of course), who found nothing in the world wrong with her. For her parents' sake, he prescribed a tonic, told them to make sure she spent time playing outdoors every day, and so on.

Neither the tonic nor the sunshine helped. Finally, beaten, Mrs. Dorson begged Mary Anne to tell her what was wrong, praying she was not going to hear a single syllable of the name Prescott. The girl's eyes filled with tears.

"I miss Mommy and Daddy," she said. "I miss Connie and Francis" (those being the Prescott children).

Mrs. Dorson thought her heart would stop or her mind would explode from her head like a bird frightened from a tree. She was starkly terrified. She summoned her husband home from his office on the double, but even when he'd heard it all, he had no better idea what to do than she did.

Was their little girl insane? Devil-possessed? They almost would have preferred the latter. They took her back to Dr. Jansen, not to be examined this time but because they didn't dare leave her at home or with a neighbor. When the doctor finally heard everything he should have heard in the first place, he didn't waste time worrying about insanity or demonic possession. Though he didn't know what was going on, he knew what had to be done, and that was to bring Mary Anne and the Prescotts together.

Faced with this idea, Mr. and Mrs. Dorson knew they'd rather have been forced to choose between the insane asylum and the exorcist. It needs to be mentioned, I'm afraid, that the Prescotts were several rungs below the Dorsons on the Vettsburg social ladder. To expose their family difficulties to people of that class was completely unthinkable (though I suspect it was rather more unthinkable for Mrs. Dorson than for her husband).

Seeing that the Dorsons would have to be brought to the idea by stages, Dr. Jansen made this suggestion. Through his contacts in the medical community, he'd check out the Prescotts and make sure they weren't the sort of people who would take advantage of this strange situation. Then if they passed this inspection, he himself would undertake to contact them.

"But what do you hope to gain from this?" Mr. Dorson asked.

"In a matter like this," the doctor said, "we're like people trapped in a cave. We can sit here and starve to death or we can set off to explore the only corridor that presents itself and hope for the best."

The Dorsons reluctantly agreed.

But there was something else Dr. Jansen wanted first, and that was to satisfy himself that he wasn't being gulled. He had a scientific turn of mind, and his first hypothesis in this case wasn't going to be that something uncanny was going on. Though he didn't say so to the Dorsons, his first hypothesis was going to be that Mary Anne was playing a mean practical joke on her parents, possibly with the collusion of one or more of the Prescotts or of someone who knew them.

During the fortnight that followed, the doctor spent two or three hours a day with either the girl or her mother. Mrs. Dorson insisted it was completely impossible to suppose that some outsider was coaching her daughter. Mary Anne wasn't one of a passel running wild; she was an only child living virtually every minute under her mother's gaze. She had two or three friends she visited occasionally, but these weren't people who would have any connection with the Prescotts, though of course the doctor was free to check this for himself—and he did.

You could see in the telling that Dr. Jansen was really getting into his role as investigator. His tests and stratagems were ingenious, subtle, and persuasive. But unless these very ordinary middle-class families were all joined in a fiendish conspiracy (and to what point?), Mrs. Dorson was right: Mary Anne had not been coached. Nor had she pieced together her picture of the Prescotts from things she'd heard or overheard at her friends' homes. The Prescotts were unknown to them all.

The doctor's next hypothesis was that the girl's babblings about the Prescotts comprised the sort of generalities that fortune tellers make their reputations on. If pressed, she'd shy away from details. If pressed harder, she'd start inventing things and soon get tangled in discrepancies and contradictions. The hypothesis foundered immediately. Mary Anne was eager to supply details of the most minute kind and was unruffled by any challenge.

The doctor's next and final hypothesis was that even if Mary Anne's lies were internally consistent, they'd collapse when compared to actuality. Of necessity, this brought him face to face with the Prescotts themselves. He proceeded with the confidence of a Grand Inquisitor, presenting himself at their house unannounced, practically accusing them of perpetrating a confidence swindle on the Dorsons. They stared at him with such open-mouthed incomprehension that he couldn't doubt what he'd already heard from others, that they were a family of thoroughly prosaic and innocuous working-class people. He apologized for having made this blustery beginning and went on to explain why he was there. When they finally understood what had been happening at the Dorson house, Dr. Jansen asked if they could imagine any ordinary way Mary Anne could have come into possession of detailed information about their lives and household arrangements. When they gave the expected answer, it was time to test the information itself.

He'd divided it into statements he could verify with his own eyes (descriptions of the house and family members) and statements only the Prescotts could verify (habits, history, and so on). It would serve no purpose to recite the process here. The material Mary Anne had provided was a mass of hits and misses, but not a hodgepodge. By the time they were finished, the character of the data was unmistakable. It was remarkably accurate—*but ten years out of date.*

Connie and Francis were no longer living with their parents, for example. Connie was married and had a home of her own. Francis had joined the army and was now a career soldier. Many of the furnishings and decorations Mary Anne had described were gone, but they'd certainly been there ten years ago.

The significance of "ten years ago" was no mystery to the Prescotts. Ten years ago they'd lost their firstborn, Natalie, to leukemia.

Now eight-year-old Mary Anne was telling anyone who would listen: "I am Natalie."

The rest of the story is rather anticlimactic and more than a little chilling. When Mary Anne finally met the Prescotts, it was eerily like a reunion. Mrs. Prescott started weeping and couldn't stop. Dr. Jensen finally had to administer a sedative and put her to bed. The Dorsons watched, frozen with horror and bewilderment, and when it was all over and they took their daughter home, they knew they'd lost her. It was an inevitable thing now. Two weeks later Mary Anne moved in with the people she considered her true parents, and that was the end of that.

News of the wonder couldn't be suppressed. With the Prescott house at its center, Vettsburg became a place of pilgrimage for thousands who wanted to believe that Mary

Anne was living proof of life after death and reincarnation. It would be nice to be able to say that the girl was unaffected by all this hullabaloo and grew into an angelic young woman, but it seems she grew into a perfectly normal young woman (one who, according to most witnesses, was a bit more than normally inclined to be sulky, spoiled, and demanding). She married twice, divorced twice, and in later life distinguished herself in no way whatever. Any sanctification that had come with being reborn in another girl's body (if that's what happened) was distinctly short-lived.

3

THIS WAS the version of the story that was put forward in the book I read at my friend's home. Later I would read other versions that were neither so tidy nor so apparently conclusive. No matter—that was later.

The uncanny events of Vettsburg opened up a new dimension of sight for me. That's the best way I can describe it. It's as if I'd been living in a sort of flatland up till then, and this book directed my gaze up into a sky I'd never suspected was there. It was not in any sense a religious experience and confirmed no religious belief on my part, since I had none. In fact, I didn't see religion as having anything to do with it and still don't. If Natalie Prescott was in fact reincarnated as Mary Anne Dorson, then this was surely a wondrous event—but no more supernatural than a caterpillar being reincarnated as a butterfly. If Natalie Prescott was in fact reincarnated as Mary Anne Dorson, then this was surely just a manifestation of a natural law whose workings are usually not manifest at all. If Natalie Prescott was in fact reincarnated as Mary Anne Dorson, then we're *all* the reincarnation of someone else—and destined to be reincarnated as someone else as well.

I slipped the book back to the maid, and that was that. The vacation came to an end, and I went back to school. Life continued as before—for another seven years, when I graduated from college and told my family I was going to work for We Live Again, a threadbare but earnest little organization devoted to reincarnation research.

They wanted to know what I meant by "work." I explained that the foundation had only two paid full-time employees, the founder, Reginald Fenshaw, and his wife, Marcia, who coordinated and compiled the fieldwork of dozens of enthusiasts working on a volunteer basis around the world. I would in effect become their first full-time fieldworker, bringing to the task not only my time and energy but the financial resources to follow up on reports anywhere in the world.

My mother thought the idea amusing and original, as if it were all an invention. My father thought it would make "an interesting way to spend the summer." In his cunning and tactful way, he was opening an avenue down which I could retreat when the project began to bore me (as he was sure it would, sooner or later). However, he had a request. Before taking up my labors on behalf of We Live Again, he asked me to talk to "Uncle Harry," who was coming to dinner the following evening. Of course I said I would.

Harold Whitaker, Ph.D., was a longtime close friend of the family (and not really any sort of uncle). I'd known him since childhood, when every adult seemed elderly, though in fact he wasn't very old even now, being perhaps in his late thirties. I seemed always to have known the man's legend better than the man himself. He'd studied at that frightfully ancient institution, Heidelberg University, and had a dueling scar on the left side of his face to prove it. He possessed several obscure academic degrees but said he favored the Ph.D. over the others because it didn't need to be explained.

For a decade after leaving school he'd been "something in the military" and wore his beautifully tailored suits as if they were uniforms. Everlastingly slim and fit, he always looked like he could rise from the dinner table and run a mile without getting winded or mussing the careful set of his fine blond hair. Now no longer in the military, he was "something in the government," and I wasn't in the least surprised to learn that recruitment was the object of our conversation.

When we were settled with our brandies in the library after dinner, he said, "I think this venture with the Reincarnation Institute sounds like fun, and I'm sure you'll learn a lot."

The family didn't care for the name of the organization, and it was quite their usual practice to reshape reality to suit themselves. Thus We Live Again had almost immediately become the more dignified Reincarnation Institute.

"But," Uncle Harry went on, "you mustn't get them too accustomed to leaning on you. In a year or two you're going to want to move on to something else."

"Yes, that's only good sense," I agreed blandly.

"I want you to be aware that anytime you want it, there's a place for you in my outfit."

"Doing what?"

"Doing what I do."

"And what's that, if I may ask?"

He shrugged. "I assumed you'd know by now that I'm in Intelligence. Or guess it."

I suppose I had guessed it, I told him, though I'm not sure I could have put the name *Intelligence* to it. "I know what you do is . . . mysterious, perhaps sinister."

"Neither one, most of the time. The government— every government everywhere and in every age—depends on men like me. On large numbers of men like me, in fact. When a leader stands in front of an audience or answers a question from the press, he almost never speaks from his own knowledge about the issues and problems of the world. For the most part, he's merely voicing *our* knowledge of those issues and problems. This is no exaggeration, I assure you."

"I believe you, though in my innocence it never occurred to me until now that this might be the case. But why me? I'm no good at languages. I have no very useful specialties."

He shook his head impatiently. "Linguists and specialists we buy in packets of ten. It's the talented generalists who are difficult to find, people with classical educations, people who are intelligent, well-bred, well-connected, and, above all, *known*."

"Known? My father is known. I hardly consider *myself* to be known."

"You're known to *me*, and that's all that matters. I can vouch for you absolutely, which is something I can never do for anyone who just walks in off the street looking for a job. He may have degrees spilling out of his pockets from the world's leading universities and letters of introduction from dozens of national heroes, but to me he's an unknown, and I wouldn't even trust him to empty the wastebaskets."

"I see. To be honest, I was expecting something like this but thought you'd just be doing it as a favor to Dad."

"Not at all. In fact, it's the other way around. I'm the one who asked for the favor, and your father granted it."

I told him I was flattered (and I was) and that I'd certainly keep the offer in mind.

"What you propose to be doing for the Institute," he went on, "could actually turn out to be excellent training for Intelligence work, I think." He paused to ponder that for a moment. "I suppose you could say that, in a sense, what you propose to be doing is Intelligence work."

I didn't particularly care to know what he meant by that, so I thanked him and adjourned the meeting *sine die*.

4

IT'S HARD TO THINK what my family, including Uncle Harry, would have made of Reggie and Marcia Fenshaw. They were so unlike anyone I'd met at home or at school that they might as well have belonged to another species. My father, I fear, would have thought them hardly different from criminals, their values were so foreign to his. They used atrociously the meager funds they had, caring nothing about money, and neglected themselves the way uncaring parents neglect their children, wearing shabby clothes, going unwashed for days, living on candy and snacks, and letting their teeth visibly rot. At the same time, if you had the slightest interest in their obsession, they would before long begin to seem to you as charming and graceful as a pair of dotty old royals pottering in their garden.

The one thing they did superlatively well was manage the data they collected from around the world. They lived for nothing else (and I've never met a happier couple in all my life).

The central feature of their system was a vast index of file cards generated by the reports they'd received over the years. If you wanted to study cases like Mary Anne Dorson's, they'd ask, "Like in what way? What feature are you looking at? Her age? The period she lived in? Her social status? The way she began to remember her last incarnation? The way her family reacted? The fact that she knew what family she belonged to in her last incarnation? The fact that this family lived nearby? The involvement of the doctor? The way her predictions were tested? The fact that the Prescotts accepted her as the reincarnation of Natalie? The fact that the rest of her life story was perfectly ordinary?" By using the card index, they could (for example) track down all the cases in which the reincarnate was able to name his or her former family. Virtually every story they had was like Mary Anne's in *some* way.

Every three or four months they rewarded their correspondents and financial supporters with a newsletter carrying the best reports received in the interval. It was, however, seldom more than four pages long, and its "best reports" were seldom worth reporting at all. In truth, it's hard to imagine anything more frustrating than the pursuit of credible evidence of reincarnation, and anyone who takes it up is putting his or her sanity at risk. The problem isn't so much that evidence isn't there but that it's invariably tainted beyond redemption by the time you get to it.

Take Mary Anne Dorson's case (which, incidentally, is

one of the very "best" on record). In the efforts he made, Dr. Jansen wasn't trying to prove the reality of reincarnation, he was just conscientiously practicing family medicine. He felt sure that the "healing" of Mary Anne could only be effected by bringing the Dorsons and the Prescotts together (and of course he was right). But the moment he succeeded in doing this, all the evidence he'd collected became worthless, and all hope of collecting further evidence disappeared forever.

If he'd been trying to build a case for reincarnation, he would have proceeded very differently. He would have immediately isolated the girl, moving her as far away as practically possible from anyone who might have knowledge of the Prescotts. Living in seclusion, she'd be wrung dry to make a record of every supposed memory of her life as Natalie, down to the smallest detail. Meanwhile, a team of scientists would descend on Vettsburg to begin work on many different fronts. Every neighbor and every child at Mary Anne's school would be examined as a possible source of her information about the Prescotts. The Prescotts themselves would be interviewed no less exhaustively to make a record of their memories of Natalie and every circumstance of their lives during the time when she was alive. When all this was done, the two records would be compiled and compared by an independent panel of scientists, and a new round of examinations would begin in order to resolve as far as possible the discrepancies and conflicts revealed. Not until all this was done would anyone dream of introducing Mary Anne to the Prescotts in the flesh—and even then it wouldn't be designed as a festivity for the girl (who by this time would probably be a young woman) but as a further and final opportunity to gather evidence.

Assembled in this way, the case would be compelling (which it otherwise certainly is not). With coincidence, blind luck, collusion, and deception decisively ruled out, skeptics would be hard pressed to suggest any other "ordinary" explanation for the wonder. If Mary Anne truly had no normal access to ten thousand items of thrice-verified information about the Prescotts during a twenty-year period before her own life began, how explain this marvel except as an instance of reincarnation?

The case as it stands convinces only those who are already convinced or who want to be convinced. When I arrived on the scene, there wasn't a single case in the files of We Live Again that did more than that. Not one even came close to doing more than that.

The Fenshaws understood this as well as anyone (and better than most of their supporters). "Someday we'll have it, though," they said.

They called it the Golden Case. The Golden Case wouldn't convert the scoffers, but it would certainly give them something to deal with, something they couldn't just wave away as superstitious nonsense.

5

I **LEARNED SOMETHING** about obsession during my time with the Fenshaws. I learned it isn't madness or even foolishness, though madness and foolishness have given it a bad name. How could anyone who wasn't obsessed compose a symphony or write a thousand-page novel? How could anyone who wasn't obsessed cross an uncharted ocean in a seventy-foot sailboat? No one sneers at people like these, but they will sneer at someone whose obsession drives them to fill a house with starving cats or to build a half-size model of the Brandenburg Gate out of matchsticks. I almost feel that someone who lives without an obsession has a poor sort of life.

I wasn't obsessed with anything when I joined the Fenshaws in Tunis, their home. The possibility of reincarnation fascinated me, but I was neither a believer nor a nonbeliever. I was there to satisfy my curiosity one way or the other, and if I'd somehow managed to do that immediately, I probably would've gone on to other things without a backward look.

One can't plausibly begin to do fieldwork without being familiar with the classic cases, and the Fenshaws had been feeding me these for a year before I arrived. In a way, these were more frustrating than the rest, because each would have been profoundly persuasive if someone had taken the trouble to demonstrate with reasonable certainty that they weren't just instances of people seeing what they wanted to see. After the event, however, no test can be run that will reveal whether what you have is gold or pyrite.

My first investigation took me to Johannesburg at the other end of the continent, where (we'd been told) there lived a young man who one morning woke up speaking a strange language that was finally determined to be ancient Persian. The young man, Rudolph Kintmacher by name, mystified all with uncanny tales of the court of Darius I, the greatest of the Achaemenid kings, which (as far as anyone could tell) were absolutely true. With this, I learned the first rule of reincarnation research, which is: If you don't investigate the silly stories, then you might as well just pack up and go home. I investigated and found it was just as silly as it sounded.

The facts (which Rudolph freely provided) bore little resemblance to what we'd heard. To begin with, he hadn't "woken up one morning" speaking Persian. He'd discovered the delight of glossolalia—speaking in tongues—long ago, while in his early teens, and had entertained friends with the trick for years before he began to take himself seriously and wonder just what language he was speaking. It was of course no language at all, but he managed to find an expert who swore it sounded just the way he'd always imagined the ancient Persians might sound. Reading up on them, Rudolph said he began to experience a powerful sense of *déjà vu*, especially when it came to the reign of the first Darius—and the rest followed as night the day.

Over the next three years I investigated four dozen cases as worthless as this one (and was on the verge of quitting) when at last I caught a glimpse of the gold.

Nine-year-old Eddie Tucker of Council Bluffs, Iowa, one morning asked his mother about the time he got sick in the boardinghouse in O'Neill. She told him he must have dreamed it, because he'd never been sick in any boarding-house anywhere. He insisted it wasn't a dream, it was some-thing he remembered from a long time ago. It didn't matter how long ago it was, she said, because they'd never lived any-where but in Council Bluffs and had never even visited a place called O'Neill. In fact, she'd never even heard of it.

The boy gave up, but only temporarily. A few hours later he came back to say he remembered that the boardinghouse had a little fish pond in the backyard, and a boy named Perry from across the street had made him a toy boat driven by a rubber band and propeller. He drew her a picture to show her what he was talking about. Her rejoinder was, "I thought you were sick at this place."

"That was later," Eddie said.

Perry had also given him a coin he'd made himself that looked just like regular money. Eddie said he could get rich if he made his own money, but Perry explained that the counterfeit cost more to make than real money, which was a little over Eddie's head at the time.

"I don't know where you're getting all this stuff," Eddie's mother said. "This never happened."

"How would you know?" Eddie riposted. "You weren't there."

"Where was I?"

"I mean Perry and I were *playing* together. You weren't out there playing with us."

"Was I in the house?"

But he didn't remember anything about that.

A few days later Eddie told his mother he'd hidden some things behind a loose brick in the foundation of the house in O'Neill, some coins, maybe. He didn't remember exactly what he'd put there, but he was sure he could find the brick.

"Do you think the things are still there?" his mother asked.

"I'll bet they are," he said.

"Why didn't you get them when we left?"

But he didn't know the answer to that.

In spite of herself, Eddie's mother had become intrigued. They got out an atlas and turned to the index for Iowa. There was an O'Brien but no O'Neill.

"Could it have been O'Brien?" she asked.

"No, I'm sure it was O'Neill."

"Well, there isn't any O'Neill."

"Try Nebraska," Eddie said—and there it was.

Checking the map, they found it was about two hundred miles northwest of Omaha, just across the river from Council Bluffs.

On the weekend, mother and boy prevailed on Dad to drive them up there. O'Neill isn't a metropolis, but it still took Eddie a while to spot the house. He wanted to head straight for the loose brick but was restrained by his parents, who knew they had to introduce themselves to the residents before starting to dismantle the foundation. The owner of the house, Thorvald Boyle, politely invited them in and listened to their story before explaining that the house still offered lodging but no longer board in this day and age. He'd acquired the house just ten years ago, when there were plenty of loose bricks in the foundation, but it had all been repointed since then. There'd also been a fish pond in the backyard, but when he bought the place it was no longer in use, having cracked one winter back in the sixties or seventies. Considering it an eyesore and not worth fixing, he'd had it ripped out.

There was no boy named Perry living across the street, but there was an old man of that name living there, in a house that had been in the Schuylkill family for something like four generations.

The Tuckers found Perry Schuylkill to be a pleasant and well-preserved eighty-six-year-old with a full head of white hair and a farmer's ruddy complexion (though he wasn't a farmer). He listened to their tale with bright-eyed interest and evident puzzlement, glancing back and forth between mother and son. When they were done, he said, "Well, this is a hell of a thing. I don't know what to think."

He stared at the boy for a long time, then began his own tale.

"There was a family that boarded across the street back in 1920 or so. I guess I was twelve or thirteen, so that would put it back in 1919 or 1920. I don't remember their name—I mean their family name. It might have been Dickens or Pickens or something like that. I can't think what business Mr. Pickens was in, but I know they didn't have a lot of money. There was a boy and a girl, though I only remember the girl, who was my age or a year or two younger. My goodness, I do remember that girl, Rita May, because she was the first love of my life, and I had the biggest crush on her you'd ever want to see. I spent a whole summer trying to impress her, and I guess maybe I did." Here Perry Schuylkill gave Eddie another long look.

"It was for her I made that nifty little boat. I remember I got the wood from a drawer-bottom of a cast-off bureau of some kind. And that coin. I remember making that for her too. She took hold of it and said, 'It feels funny, sort of slick, like it's got oil on it.'"

"I remember that," Eddie said. "And you said, 'That's just from the process,' or something like that."

Mr. Schuylkill nodded, and Eddie's mother burst into tears, for no reason she could ever cogently explain.

At the end of the summer, Mr. Schuylkill went on, Rita May fell ill. He thought it might have been rheumatic fever but couldn't be sure. "I didn't care what it was," he said. "I just wanted it to go away. But it didn't, and my precious love passed away in a little room under the fourth-floor eaves of that house right over there. I can show it to you if you like. I'm sure Mr. Boyle wouldn't mind."

But Eddie's mother wanted no part of that.

After their visit to O'Neill, Eddie dredged up a few more details of his life as Rita May Pickens, but he later admitted that even he wasn't sure whether he'd dredged them up or made them up.

It took two years for rumors of the case to reach our ears—a usual sort of interval—but Perry Schuylkill was still alive and alert, as were all the others. It all checked out. All the principals and witnesses seemed guileless, earnest types who had nothing to gain from deceiving me or anyone else.

It was a classic, but what did it actually amount to? Having a fish pond in the backyard was hardly unique to that one house. It would have been different if it had been a pagoda or a pyramid. The loose brick was no longer there to be counted, so it all comes down to a toy boat, a counterfeit coin, and a recollection of being sick in a town with a name that, to my surprise, proved to be unique. I was unable to find even one more O'Neill (or anything like it) anywhere else in the world.

It wasn't much, but I'd seen the glint of gold with my own eyes and could no longer doubt its existence. I wanted to see more—and in extractable, weighable, usable amounts.

The obsession was finally upon me.

Seven more years flew by, and by the time I next saw gold everyone had gotten used to writing year dates starting with 20 instead of 19.

6

AFTER A HUNDRED DISAPPOINTMENTS, you learn not to let your nerves start sizzling every time a new report comes in. You play it cool, because, after all, you know that no matter how good it looks, it's probably just going to end up being more of the usual garbage. But it was hard to play it cool in the case of Mallory Hastings, age twenty-eight, of Oneonta, New York.

As events had been reconstructed, she skidded off the road late one night during a snowstorm. She couldn't manage to get the car back on the road but figured a passing car would soon stop to offer assistance. In any event, she stayed in the car with the engine running, not suspecting that the exhaust system had taken a hit and was now leaking carbon monoxide into the passenger compartment. Luckily someone did come along to assist before long, but not before Mallory had lost consciousness. She was rushed to a hospital, where she lay in a coma for two days before beginning to show signs of returning consciousness.

Her mother and a nurse were at the bedside ready to reassure her that all was well, but when Mallory opened her eyes and took her first look around, she reacted with abject panic, which seemed to get worse the more they tried to reassure her, until the nurse summoned a doctor to administer a sedative. The doctor didn't want to give her any kind of sedative at this point and tried his own hand at calming her down, with no more success than the others had had. Finally he decided that administering the sedative was going to be the lesser of the two evils.

When everything grew calm again, they tried to figure out what had gone wrong. Mrs. Hastings had never seen her daughter behave this way. The doctor rechecked the X rays, confirming that there was no head injury—not even a bruise.

The nurse asked them if they'd seen the gesture Mallory had made repeatedly with her right hand. Now that she'd drawn their attention to it, they did remember it.

"It looked like something in sign language," the nurse offered.

Mrs. Hastings replied indignantly that her daughter didn't know sign language.

"All the same, that's what it looked like," the nurse insisted.

"Why on earth would she be using sign language?" Mallory's mother wanted to know.

"Well, you notice she didn't say anything."

"That's true," the doctor said, "but it can't have anything

to do with her signing. If she didn't know the language in the first place, she certainly didn't learn it while she was in a coma!"

When Mallory began to stir again a few hours later, the doctor, nurse, and mother were again on hand, but this time Mallory was in restraints that would prevent her from injuring herself.

"It's all right, Mallory," her mother said, stroking her daughter's forehead. "Everything's fine. You're fine, the car's fine, everything's going to be all right."

But even before she opened her eyes, Mallory was writhing in agony.

"I'm going to make a suggestion," the doctor said hastily. "Let's leave Mallory alone for a while and let her collect herself at her own pace." He dragged the others outside and stationed himself in front of the door, leaving it open a crack in order to observe. "She's calming down," he said after a minute. Then, after another minute: "She's got her eyes open and is looking around the room. She seems fine now."

But just then, without changing expression, she emitted a terrific groan, which seemed to startle her as much as anyone else. She looked around wildly and again briefly struggled against her restraints before settling down.

"*Gwawk*," she said after a moment—or something like it. Once again she seemed as surprised as anyone else at this accomplishment.

"What's *wrong* with her?" Mrs. Hastings demanded plaintively.

"I haven't the slightest idea," the doctor said.

"Has she lost her voice?"

"On the contrary, she seems to be finding it."

"Are you saying *that's* her voice?"

The doctor gave her a stern medical glare. "Mrs. Hastings, I'm not saying *anything* at this point. You know as much as I do—and a great deal more, since you've known her from birth!"

"But you've got to do something!"

"What the devil would you suggest, Mrs. Hastings? Do you want me to sedate her again?"

"No," the woman said, suitably crushed.

"Well, I do have a suggestion," said the nurse. "You're a man, and Mrs. Hastings is upset. I'd like to go in there alone and see if I can talk to her."

The doctor checked the crack again and watched for half a minute. "All right. That's probably a good idea. Just go slow with her."

"I'm not an *idiot*," the nurse said, and pushed her way in.

When she caught Mallory's eye, she put her index finger to her lips in the universal "no talking" gesture. Mallory looked at her gravely, then lifted her chained right hand as if to reply. The restraint visibly upset her, and the nurse released her from it. Then she offered her some water, which she took gratefully through a straw.

In a quiet tone the nurse said, "Can you hear me all right?"

Mallory nodded.

"Can you speak?"

Mallory shook her head, then shrugged and nodded, then shook her head again.

"You don't know whether you can speak or not, is that it?"

Mallory nodded emphatically. And lifted her right hand

to sign rapidly. The nurse glanced at the door, hoping that the gesture had been caught.

"Do you speak sign language?"

Mallory nodded.

"I'll get someone here who talks sign. Will that be okay?"

Again she nodded.

The nurse thought for a moment then again asked if Mallory could hear her.

Mallory signed wildly, pointing to her ears and to the nurse's lips, then shook her head.

Inspired, the nurse put her hand over her mouth and asked the question again.

The young woman began thrashing in her bed.

"Okay, okay," the nurse said. "I understand. You're reading my lips, right?"

Mallory nodded.

Once a sign reader had been brought in, the situation became clearer—and simultaneously more mysterious.

Mallory could hear but didn't understand what she heard. The reason? She was deaf. No one seemed able to follow this. How could she be deaf if she heard what was being said? If she could hear it, why couldn't she understand it?

Because she was deaf.

The translator explained it this way. "The last thing she remembers before she woke up in this bed is being deaf. She could read lips, but, because she was deaf, she didn't know what sounds were being produced by those lips. So when she started hearing those sounds here today, she didn't know what to make of them. And she still doesn't. She can hear us talking, but it's just gibberish unless she uses her eyes to read our lips."

"This is ridiculous," Mrs. Hastings declared emphatically. "There has never been a single thing wrong with Mallory's hearing. She studied violin, for God's sake!"

"Have you ever studied violin, Mallory?" asked the translator. When Mallory was finished signing, the translator turned to the others and said, "She wants to know who Mallory is."

Mrs. Hastings swayed and would've fallen if the doctor hadn't grabbed her.

7

EVERY MEDICAL SPECIALIST within two hundred miles wanted a chance to solve the mystery, which only seemed to deepen as time went on. As far as anyone could tell, Mallory's ears and vocal apparatus worked as well as anyone else's and always had done so. Physically, she was a normal, healthy young woman. No grounds, neurological or psychological, could be found for what everyone understood to be a condition of amnesia. Emotionally, she was an impenetrable conundrum.

Teams of speech therapists worked with her daily to build a connection in her mind between the spoken language she was hearing and the facial language she was seeing, and, of course, to teach her how to speak (again). She was indifferent to their efforts, often ignoring them completely or preferring to sleep. She settled into hospital life and seemed to have no interest in "recovering" or resuming a "normal life."

Mallory had been a librarian, second in command at Oneonta's main library. When "reminded" of this, she shrugged. She'd been an avid reader of murder mysteries, and a friend brought her the latest from one of her favorite authors. She flipped through the pages and set it aside. But then it seemed to give her an idea.

She asked for a book with pictures in it—but she asked in sign, which her friend didn't understand. A speech therapist was called in to translate, but he refused.

"Mallory can tell us what she has on her mind," he said. "Can't you, Mallory? There's nothing wrong with your voice, and you've got to start using it to get the things you want. That's what it's there for."

They could see she was tempted to tell them to go to hell, but then, after thinking about it some more, she evidently decided she really wanted that book.

"I want a book with pictures," she said—or at least intended to say. She had to make several trials before it was intelligible.

"What kind of pictures?" her friend asked.

"Pictures of people."

"What kind of people?"

"Many," Mallory said. "Many."

"I don't understand."

"Different kinds. All different."

Her friend still didn't quite fathom what she was getting at but promised to look around and see what she could find.

The therapist said, "Wouldn't you like to see a newspaper? Or a magazine?"

"No!"

That was one word she'd mastered.

Both of Mallory's parents were profoundly distressed, of
course, but Mrs. Hastings was the more eloquent of the two,
threatening alternately to sue the hospital into oblivion if
they didn't fix whatever they'd done wrong and to flay her
daughter alive if she didn't stop playing the fool. After four
days, hospital officials tried to explain to her that there was
no reason why Mallory couldn't go home, but she was obviously not going to do so if Mrs. Hastings continued to ter-
rorize her.

The woman said, "Why, Mallory knows very well I
wouldn't harm her!"

She stubbornly refused to hear anyone say that Mallory
evidently knew no such thing.

Mallory's friend returned with an armload of coffee-table
books filled with pictures of people—movie stars, fashion
models, musicians, workers, farmers, people at sporting
events, at political rallies, at concerts, on holiday, in court-
rooms, on street corners. Mallory went through them like a
threshing machine, giving each page no more than a glance,
then furiously swept them all off the bed and buried her
head under a pillow.

"What is it, Mallory?" her friend asked, stunned. "What
are you looking for?"

Mallory shook her head wordlessly.

Her friend gathered up the books and was about to leave when it occurred to her to wonder if Mallory wanted to keep them. After voicing the question, she realized she was wasting her breath, since Mallory probably couldn't comprehend what she was hearing. She carefully set the books down on the bed, close enough to Mallory that she couldn't avoid feeling them against her hip. With a convulsive twist of her body, Mallory sent them flying off the bed a second time.

Her friend gathered them up again and left without saying another word. At this point (she would later say), she knew the woman in the bed "wasn't Mallory." Mallory, she insisted, would never behave that way, not in a million years.

8

BECAUSE THE New York newspapers carried the story (in a predictably souped-up version), we heard about it in Tunis almost immediately, and I took the first available flight out. I might have saved myself the trouble, since hospital officials saw no reason to let me in, and Mr. and Mrs. Hastings turned up their noses as soon as I explained who I was. Members of the sensationalist press had standing, but I was persona non grata (and a foreigner as well, despite my famous name and the fact that I'd grown up within sight of Central Park).

Leaving a local associate to stand watch at the hospital, I took the opportunity to pay a visit to the ancestral home, arriving unannounced, as I always did, because it seemed not to make the slightest difference whether my parents knew I was coming or not. They greeted me as if I'd been gone a week, when in fact it had been close to four years.

"What good luck," Mother said cheerily. "Uncle Harry's coming to dinner. He'll be so glad to see you. He always asks for news of you."

"Does he really?" I replied, mildly surprised to hear that he hadn't given up on me by now.

Mother liked doing things in the baronial style to which our means presumably entitled us, so dinner was like a state affair, for which everyone dressed, including me. My room was untouched, with racks of clothes that I'd left behind, and I had my pick of four virtually identical suits of evening wear. Mother had come along to advise, and tutted when she saw them, for naturally they were no longer quite in the pink of fashion. I caught her eyeing my waist to see if the measurements on record with my tailor needed to be adjusted and knew that a new array of dinner jackets would be awaiting me on my next visit. I also knew there was nothing in the world I could say that would dissuade her from ordering them.

Dinner was charming and fun, and I heard all my parents' news, which is hardly ever really news. The old things the very rich do are so stupendously wonderful that they almost never have to trouble themselves to do new ones.

Naturally they wanted to hear all about my adventures, which they listened to with only the slightest air of condescension. They saw no great difference between someone like Rudolph Kintmacher of Johannesburg and Eddie Tucker of Council Bluffs, though Mother would say "What fun!" about the first and "How sad!" about the second, treating them both like elaborate fictions cooked up for her amusement.

Uncle Harry, taking it a bit more seriously, wanted to know what I made of it all. "Do you really think Rita May's soul lives in Eddie Tucker's body?"

"I truly don't know what to think," I told him. "Can you come up with another explanation?"

While he was pondering this, my father shifted in his chair in a way that reliably summons the attention of the table and said, "What I can't see is that it matters a damn. Just for the sake of argument, let's say there is such a thing as a soul animating my body. And let's suppose you could certify beyond doubt that this identical soul once animated the body of Julius Caesar. Isn't that the theory, more or less?"

"Yes, more or less."

"Well, what difference could it possibly make? Why would anyone care, since I don't have access to the memories of Julius Caesar?"

"But that's the whole point," I said. "Suppose you woke up one morning and found that you *did* have access to his memories."

"Then I hope someone would have the good sense to pack me off to the loony bin," he said, and concluded the meal (and the discussion) by tossing his napkin onto the table in front of him.

As hard as I tried to avoid being sequestered with Harry, he tried harder to corner me, so we finally ended up *tête-à-tête.*

"I hope you won't mind if I'm blunt," he said.

"I'll brace myself for it, Uncle Harry."

He frowned, not quite sure he liked my jaunty tone. "It's just that I wouldn't want to see you lose yourself in this reincarnation business," he said. "I've seen it happen to other men. They start a thing as a hobby, then it swallows them up. They come to a point where they can't think of anything else, can't get involved with anything else."

"Aren't you swallowed up in your work?"

"Yes," he said, without hesitation. "And if I weren't, I'd be useless to it."

"And the difference?"

"The difference is, Jason, that this reincarnation thing is going to come to nothing. You can spend a lifetime on it—six lifetimes, if you like—and in the end you'll be exactly what you are right now, a voice crying in the wilderness, with no one listening and no one caring. You're trying to prove something that's no more susceptible of proof than ghosts or second sight or life after death. When you're all finished, it'll be just the way it is now: The believers will believe and the unbelievers won't, and your work won't have made a particle of difference."

"Whereas yours does."

"Walk with me a week, Jason, and you'll *know* it does."

His earnestness made it impossible for me to be indignant. He wasn't trying to insult me or to hurt my feelings.

"What would you like me to say?" I asked him.

"That you'll give some serious thought to what I'm telling you."

"All right, I'll do that."

He confessed he couldn't ask for more than that.

• • •

The next morning I located some of my mother's stationery and went to work on a letter.

Dear Mallory (if I may):

My name will mean nothing to you. I suspect that all the names of the people who are haunting your life at the moment mean nothing to you. But although you don't know me (and I don't know you), I'm going to make three important guesses about you.

First: You're not Mallory Hastings at all. You may or may not know who you really are, but you definitely know you're not Mallory Hastings, no matter what the people around you are saying.

Second: You don't know how you got where you are. The last thing you remember is that you were someone else and somewhere else.

Third: You're afraid to speak the truth to the people around you. You don't know what would happen if you told them that you're not Mallory Hastings and that your last memory is of being someone else, somewhere else.

So now, Mallory (as I'll have to call you till I know your real name), please tell me how I've done with my guesses.

The phone listed at the bottom of this stationery is answered twenty-four hours a day. I'm sure the people at the hospital will let you make a long-distance call if you ask them. Or you can write to me at the address below. That'll take a little longer, but do whatever is comfortable for you.

I hope you'll believe me when I say I understand what you're going through and only want to help. And I can help, I'm sure of that.

Sincerely,
Jason Tull, Jr.

At this point, I'd learned none of the specifics of Mallory's situation, but I knew from experience that my "guesses" were virtual certainties. It's axiomatic in paranormal research that the honest run into a wall of disbelief while deliberate hoaxers win ready acceptance.

9

Dear Mr. Tull,

Thanks for your letter, and I really mean that. To this drowning woman, it was a lifeline. It gave me the incentive I needed to work with the speech therapists here—or I should say it gave me a <u>reason</u> to work with them. When I received your letter, I desperately wanted to call you, but I knew I wouldn't be able to make myself understood over the phone. I was afraid you'd think I was an idiot and give up on me, so I really went to work and will be much improved by the time this reaches you.

You scored three out of three right on your guesses. Because I'm afraid of the people here (and especially the woman who insists she's my mother), I didn't show your letter to anyone. But I wanted to find out why you wrote to me, so I asked one of the nurses if she'd ever heard of you.

She said, oh sure, but the man she was thinking of was your father. She didn't know anything about Jason Tull, Jr.

So these are the questions on my mind right now. How were you able to make your three guesses? You say you want to help me, but how? Did someone put a spell on me that you can undo? I hope you don't mind my asking. Anyway, the real question is, what next? What do you have in mind? And what should I do, if anything?

You've already helped, by giving me something to hope for, and I thank you for that.

Mallory (for now)

Dear Mallory (and please make it Jason):

I don't at all mind your asking how I knew and how I can help but would rather answer these questions in person if I may. This brings me to what comes next and to what you can do.

What's next is for me to visit you in the hospital. What you can do is tell the people there, first, that I'm coming, and, second, that you want me to be passed through (which I was not the last time I was there). I feel sure you can insist on this. It isn't as though you're a ten-year-old. You're an adult and certainly have a right to choose your own associates.

The hospital people may feel obliged to tell Mrs. Hastings about this. You can ask them not to if you feel like it, but there's probably no way to stop them.

Since Mrs. Hastings doesn't understand the situation, she's trying to do the next best thing, which is to control it. She may very well perceive me as a threat to her control and try to block me from seeing you. If it looks like this is going to happen, then you'd better phone me. If necessary, I can arrive with a battalion of lawyers to persuade everyone that they don't want to get into a position where they seem to be holding you against your will. As I understand it, the hospital's stance is that there's no reason why you can't go home, so that should settle the matter for them. But I don't know what "home" means. Did Mallory live with her parents or somewhere else? It won't hurt to have the answers to questions like these. You presumably have a driver's license, and that'll have an address on it.

This letter should be in your hands in two or three days at the most. I'll present myself at the hospital on the fourth day. If there's some problem, phone me. Otherwise, I'll see you soon.

Jason

Mrs. Hastings evidently decided (or was persuaded) that yielding gracefully was going to work better for her than drawing a battle line across the hospital steps, so I was waved through to the elevators as if I were a kinsman. The press had published no pictures of Mallory, so I was unprepared for what I saw when I pushed my way through the door to her room: a flawless Aryan snow maiden—milky skin, eyes as blue as the Mediterranean, and hair as yellow as the sun. I suppose I was gawking a bit when the girl in the bed glanced up from her book, with her wounded eyes and chaste, narrow lips making her look rather more like an elfin child than a woman of twenty-six. She returned my gaze for a moment, then produced an almost imperceptible shrug.

"You fuckhead," she said flatly. "Go home and die."

Bewildered, I looked over my shoulder to see who she was talking to, but I was alone. She was talking to me.

I said, "I'm Jason Tull."

"I didn't think you were Chester Morris."

Blinking stupidly, I asked her who Chester Morris was.

She sighed and went back to her book.

I stood there for a minute then asked what I'd done wrong.

"You were born," she said without looking up. "That's where it began."

I couldn't imagine what she meant by that, but I felt I had to make a stab at it. "You mean . . . it's something about my family. About being born a Tull."

"Forget it," she said, tossing her book aside. "Sit down and we'll start over."

Several sets of muscles wanted to accept the invitation, but I held them in check. "I think I'd rather start over on a more even footing than this, Mallory. Give me a call when you're ready to talk." I turned to go, and she said, "Wait a minute."

I turned back and waited.

She sat for a moment staring into the middle distance. Then, as if offering a demonstration, she raised a hand and deliberately raked the side of her face with her nails, leaving four livid tracks.

"Get that?" she asked.

I admitted I didn't.

"This isn't me."

"I don't understand."

"You stood there admiring this face, but you weren't admiring *me*. You were acting just like all the rest of them."

"I'm sorry."

"I've been a woman," she said. "I know how it goes. A man tells a woman, 'You're very beautiful,' and she's supposed to feel like he's saying something about *her*, as though that beauty runs clear through her. But if you tell me *I'm* beautiful, you're just talking about some bones and skin and hair that don't even belong to me. It's like you take it for granted that *I'll* feel complimented if you stand there admiring some *other* woman's face."

"I understand. If someone says Mallory's beautiful, this has nothing to do with you. You don't own that face."

"That's right."

"But you *do* own it, you know. It's yours now, for the rest of your life. You might as well get used to accepting the compliment, to saying, 'Yes, you're right, I *am* beautiful.'"

She gave her head a little shake. "You can't know that. Maybe next week I'll be gone just the way Mallory's gone."

"No," I said on my way to a chair, "that's no more likely to happen to you than it is to me."

"But it *did* happen."

I sat down and crossed my legs, making myself at home. "It did happen—once—virtually a miracle, something that happens once every billion man-years."

"What do you mean by that?"

"If there are a billion people on the earth, we experience a billion man-years of human life every year. And that's about how often this happens—and why it's hardly likely to happen twice to the same person."

"All right, I can see that." She paused, momentarily lost in thought, and I had a glimpse of the calm intensity that would come to her naturally when the present turmoil and confusion subsided. "But tell me this," she said at last. "Where did Mallory go? I've got to know that, because I feel like a murderer. Where is Mallory?"

I lifted a finger and pointed it straight at her. "There is Mallory."

"I'M GOING TO *explain* the theory," I went on, "because theory is all we have. What's happened to you has happened before, hundreds of times at least. I, personally, have met half a dozen people it's happened to, and this is how we explain it until we have a better way. Every human is animated by a soul, which departs the body at death and subsequently migrates to another body, which it animates at conception or sometime soon after. In this new incarnation, the soul has no recollection of its previous incarnation—or of any of its previous incarnations. At least not ordinarily. But once in a very great while someone will spontaneously begin to recollect details of a previous incarnation—name, family, place of residence, and so on. Most often, memories of the person's past incarnation exist side by side with those of the present incarnation. But sometimes, even more rarely, memories of the past incarnation overwhelm those of the present incarnation—supplant them, blot them out. And of course that's what's happened in your case. You haven't *murdered* Mallory, you've just lost all memory of *being* Mallory."

Looking stunned, she shook her head. "You mean I was born into this body. Despite everything my memory tells me, you're saying I have as much business being here as Mallory did."

"That's right. The break is in your memories, not in the person you experience as yourself."

"That's bullshit," she said. "Excuse me, but it is. The person I experience as myself is exactly what's broken."

She had a point, which I had to acknowledge. "Try it this way," I said. "Many people experience amnesia for one reason or another, usually as a result of a head injury. I assume you know that."

"I guess so. Go ahead."

"And what usually happens in these cases is that they remember nothing of their past at all. It's a blank, right?"

"Right."

"Let's say this happens to someone called Tom Williams. He gets hit in the head by a falling roof beam, and when he wakes up in the hospital, his mind is a total blank. He doesn't know his name, doesn't recognize his wife or his children, and so on."

"Okay."

"So what do you think? Has he ceased to be Tom Williams? I don't know about you, but I'd have to say not. He's still Tom Williams, even if he can't remember *being* Tom Williams."

"Okay, I can see that."

"But now let's look at a much rarer case. In this one-in-a-billion case, the amnesiac wakes up in the hospital, but her mind isn't a blank. Instead, she has a complete set of memories of being someone else. That's what happened to you, isn't it?"

She nodded.

"Who were you in that previous life, Mallory? What was your name?"

"Gloria MacArthur."

"So that's the difference between you and Tom Williams. When he woke up, he was nobody, and when you woke up, you were Gloria MacArthur. But by any measure anyone can make, he was still Tom Williams and you're still Mallory Hastings."

"I can see all that, but . . . "

"Yes?"

"I just can't buy into this soul business."

"Neither can I."

Her eyes widened at that. "I don't get it. What are you saying?"

"I'm saying that what I've given you is a theory, a way of explaining something that happens—and it's the best I have at the moment. Give me a better one that doesn't involve this 'soul business,' and I'll embrace it like a shot, believe me. But most people just throw out the baby with the bath water."

"Meaning what?"

"Many people are unable to distinguish the theory from the phenomenon it tries to explain. They figure that if the theory is nonsense, then the phenomenon must be nonsense too. If I tell people that Mallory Hastings is the reincarnation of Gloria MacArthur, they'll just say I'm crazy."

"You mean, according to them, I'm faking all this."

"Or imagining it. Maybe you just wanted a new life for yourself—were fed up with being second banana at the library." That won a hesitant sort of smile, as if smiling were something she'd forgotten along with all the rest.

"So what do we do now?" Gloria/Mallory asked.

"What do you *want* to do?"

"It's funny," she said after thinking for a moment. "I needed to be rescued."

"You evidently felt you couldn't get out of here under your own power."

"That's right."

"And this is what you want to do? Get out of here?"

"You bet."

"And go where?"

The question seemed to perplex her. Finally she said, "I don't understand what you're doing here. I know why *I* wanted you to be here, but I don't know why *you* wanted to be here. What is it you want?"

"I work for a nonprofit organization that studies events like this, events that seem to demonstrate the reality of reincarnation. In your case, I'm here to try to verify the memories of your former life. Working together, we'll try to find the person who acquired those memories during her life as Gloria MacArthur."

She emitted a little sigh of exasperation. "Why can't you talk like ordinary people? 'The person who acquired those memories'? What's that mean?"

"I'm sorry. You're right, I'm being a little cryptic. Where did you grow up as Gloria MacArthur?"

Darting me a suspicious look, she asked why I wanted to know that.

"Gloria MacArthur is—or was—a real person who lived sometime in the past. Together, the two of us are going to track her down and find out how closely your memories match the reality of her life."

"No, we're not," she said simply but definitely.

"We're not?"

"No."

"I see," I said, getting up out of my chair. "Well, let's get you discharged, then we can go from there. Did you by any chance find out where Mallory Hastings lives?"

By this time, the hospital's personnel no longer bothered to be amazed at the things Mallory didn't know about herself. We asked for a map and driving instructions, and they provided them. When we got into the car I'd driven up from Manhattan, Mallory sank into the passenger seat, pulled her coat collar up around her face, and let me drive, looking neither right nor left as we traveled to a prim little gated community north of the city, where she owned a prim little condominium. Using the keys from her purse, I let us in and turned on the lights in the gathering twilight. Mallory followed me into the living room, glanced around, and shuddered like a prisoner being led into the cell where she'd be spending the rest of her life.

It was in fact an appalling place, decorated in a style of meaningless perfection, as if everything had been ordered from a catalog of unobjectionable furnishings, neither too dowdy nor too elegant—a vase of a certain size here, a picture of a certain type there, all as indicated in the accompanying diagram.

"I can't stand it," Mallory said.

"You don't have to. You can throw it all out and start over."

Predictably, she shook her head.

"You should check your telephone messages," I told her.

"How do I do that?"

I showed her, and we learned that Mallory Hastings had a wide circle of nice-sounding friends, who left nice messages wishing her a speedy recovery. We also learned she had an ex-boyfriend, Phil, who couldn't understand why his calls were being ignored but who eventually got tired of asking. There seemed to be no point in worrying about any of them.

"You should probably let your mother know that you're home, however," I said.

"She's *not* my mother."

So we hadn't made any progress on that score.

"I don't want to stay here," she said. She still hadn't taken off her coat, hadn't sat down.

"Don't be childish," I told her, not meanly, just letting her know I didn't plan to pamper her forever.

She looked around once more and said, "Help me get rid of at least some of this crap."

We stripped the place of everything that would move, then went on a shopping spree to replace it.

No question about it—Gloria's tastes were not Mallory's. She wanted nothing that was handsome, nothing that hinted of refinement. No one was to mistake her for a genteel young lady with conventional good taste. She bought quickly, almost randomly, explaining that she'd find things she liked better later, and when we got it home, she wouldn't rest till it was all in place.

The effect was different (and in its way no less appalling), but she declared she could live with it for the time being.

It was nine o'clock, and I was hungry, as I supposed she was. I told her we could probably find a restaurant that was still serving, but she said she was tired, and that was that. As a concession, she offered me whatever I could find to eat in the fridge and the use of her sofa. I told her I was booked into a hotel downtown. It was far from grand, but, to be honest, I was looking forward to it. I needed a rest from the reincarnated Gloria MacArthur.

I WOKE the next morning with the sudden, clear presentiment that I was taking on far too much with this woman. Now that I had a foot in the door, I needed to get her reconnected with her family, otherwise I was in danger of ending up as a sort of unofficial guardian, or something worse (though I wasn't sure what that might be).

I had visions of my arriving at her condominium to find her gone, God knows where, and it would all be my fault. I'd be accused of murder, kidnapping, or running a white slavery ring. In fact, she wasn't gone when I arrived, but the actuality wasn't a whole lot better than the fantasy. Before she even had the door all the way open, she was screaming at me.

"I can't stand this, I've got to get out of here!"

"Have you had anything to eat?"

"I'm not talking about eating, I'm talking about getting out of here!"

Still standing outside the front door, I gave her a confident, manly smile and said, "Look, Mallory, we can do both those things. Let's get out of here and go find someplace to have breakfast, okay? You may not need sustenance, but I do."

"All right, I'll get a coat—but don't come in."

"Why not?"

"Because you'll sit down or something."

So I stood there on the stoop till she was ready. I was so flummoxed that it didn't even occur to me that I could have waited in the car, where I would have looked and felt marginally less ridiculous.

Though she claimed to have no appetite, she attacked a plate of eggs and bacon as if she hadn't eaten in a week. Unfortunately, having a full stomach didn't seem to improve her outlook a whole lot. I was beginning to wonder if Gloria MacArthur had died in childhood. It would explain Mallory's evident lack of maturity, but I hesitated to ask, knowing how suspicious she was of every question.

It came to me that a heavy irony was at work here. For the first time ever, I'd made my way into a case early enough to safeguard the evidence, but precisely because I was so early, I couldn't get anywhere *near* the evidence. The subject was preoccupied with more elemental matters, and it was going to be days, if not weeks, before she was ready to help me with the investigation I'd come to make.

I asked what she was thinking about her future.

"What do you mean?" she asked in reply—evasively, I felt, since she was plainly thinking about nothing else.

"Well, for example, do you plan to go back to your job at the library?"

"Don't be stupid," she said. "I wouldn't even know where to find the goddamn place, much less do the work."

"Then how are you going to make a living?"

"There's some money in the bank," she told me. "Mallory was a saver."

"That's nice. It gives you some time to think."

"Yeah," she agreed sullenly.

"Your family may be able to help."

She gave me a disgusted look. "My family's dead."

"Mallory has a family, and as far as they're concerned, you're Mallory. You've got to get used to that. It's a fact that's not going to go away."

"It can go away as far as I'm concerned."

"What have you got against them?"

"They're—" she started, then caught herself.

"They're what?"

"Weasels. Warts."

I wanted to tell her they couldn't possibly be as bad as all that, but I knew I'd be wasting my breath.

We were on our third postprandial cup of coffee. I had no idea what was supposed to come next, and she didn't seem disposed to enlighten me. I considered telling her I was going back to New York City and she could get in touch when she felt like it, but I was afraid she'd think that was fine.

Finally I said, "I take it you don't want to go back to your condominium."

"That's right, I don't."

"Then what do you want to do?"

"I want to find someplace else to live."

"What kind of place?"

On that point she was standing mute.

"Where do you want to look? Here in Oneonta?"

"What's the point of that?" she wanted to know.

"I don't know. It's here, it's handy, and, like it or not, you've got all sorts of connections here, including a bank account and references."

She shook her head.

I signaled to the waitress for the check. "Look, Mallory, I'm glad to help, but I can't read your mind. We can't just sit here drinking coffee for the rest of our lives."

"I know," she said, giving me an anxious look. "What would happen if we went to New York City?"

"What would happen? We'd be there instead of here."

"Then let's go there."

At last it was my turn to shake my head. "Maybe someday, Mallory, but not now. Not unless you get together with your parents and let them know what's going on. I'm not taking you outside Oneonta unless they're in on it."

She glared at me and said, "You're a fink."

"A what?"

"A fink. Don't you know what a fink is?"

"No, I'm afraid I don't."

She shrugged. "I guess it's slang of a different generation. It means you're on the side of the big shots. You know which side your bread's buttered on."

"You mean because I want your parents to know where you're going?"

cks in the eastern section of the city—and this dismal
e, faced with warehouses and factories, seemed to strike
llory as especially promising.

"You're not going to find any housing down here," I told her.

"I'm not looking for housing."

"Then what? Are you planning to open a paper mill?"
She withered me with a scornful look.

After taking down the numbers of several agents with
perty in the area, we were heading off to find a phone
en we accidently stumbled on a building that satisfied her
rt's desire. Unlike most of its neighbors, it was a single-
ry structure, concrete block, with tall lattice windows,
ertised to be twenty-four hundred square feet. If the peel-
sign on the facade was to believed, it had once been home
Wilson Mackie Wire Products.

"You can't seriously think of *living* there, Mallory. It
n't have anything like a kitchen or a bath."

"I know how to live without a kitchen or a bath," she said
kly.

It wouldn't be exactly true to say that that was that. The
estate agent was happy enough to show us the building,
ch was surprisingly clean inside, but balked at giving her
ase. He wanted either six months' rent in advance or a
igner—"a grownup," as he undiplomatically put it.

'Not me," I said, when I saw her gaze swivel in my direc-
. "Not a chance."

She thought a moment, then reached for her checkbook.

"You shouldn't do that," I told her. "Contact your par-
. Let them cosign with you."

She hesitated, but only for a fraction of a second, then
te him out a check for six months' rent.

"That's right. You won't take my side against them."

"Why should I, for God's sake? You shouldn't be making
enemies of them—and I certainly won't *help* you make enemies of them."

"All right," she said, getting up. "I'll stay in fucking
Oneonta."

①②

"SO," I SAID, once we were back in the car
staying in fucking Oneonta mean? Do you w
paper and look for rentals or shall I just drive
and down the next?"

"Let's look around downtown," she replied.

Oneonta is one of the ancient cities of th
proud of the fact that it has remained steadfas
old-fashioned. When its elderly brick build
they aren't so much replaced as re-created, and
the venerable bandstand on Main Street has b
the outset (though by now every stick of it
been replaced many times over).

A railroad freight line roughly parallels Ma
blocks to the south, and a Railroad Avenu

It was a strange development, but it had its points. On the lease, Mallory had acknowledged having a residence (her condominium), her parents (as references), and a place of employment (the library). Despite her habit of denial, she was willy-nilly beginning to forge some links to the present.

Mallory had different ways of being silent, depending on whether she was furious, just wanted to be left alone, was self-absorbed, or was uneasy about how her next move was going to be received. The silence that swallowed us up as we headed back to the condominium was of the last type, I sensed, and she confirmed it when we arrived.

She no longer needed my services. She was ready to take up life on her own. She wanted to be left alone, at least for the time being.

"It's going to take a lot of work to make that wire factory livable," I told her. "I'll be glad to help, and it'll go a lot faster with two pairs of hands."

She shook her head. "You're always dragging me back, always telling me what I've got to do and what I can't do. Every single thing you think I should do is something I don't want to do, and every single thing I want to do is something you think I shouldn't do."

I had to admit she had a point.

"You just wear me down," she went on.

"I'm sorry," I said, meaning it.

"You've got to—" Mallory paused, blinked, and made a sign with her right hand. "I can't think of the word, the expression." She made the sign a couple more times, watching as if the hand itself might reveal the word she wanted. "It means, like, you're paddling the boat north and I'm paddling it south. All we're doing is wearing each other out."

"I understand what you're saying, and I agree to a certain extent, but I don't think you're being fair. You wanted to get out of the hospital, and I helped you with that, didn't I?"

"Yes, that's true."

"You wanted to redecorate your apartment, and I helped you with that, didn't I?"

"Yes."

"You wanted a new place to live, and I helped you with that too. Everything you've gotten done in the past two days is something I helped with."

"Yeah, all right," she said, disgusted. "But this is what I want to do next. I want to put together my own pad. I suppose that's dated too—'my pad.'"

"It is, but I understand what you mean, from the context."

"Will you help me do that?"

"Do what?"

"I said I want to put together my own pad. Will you help me do that?"

"Yes."

"Then go away for a week. This is something I've got to do by myself. I *want* to do it by myself. Can't you dig that?"

I smiled, feeling oddly flattered to be initiated in this way into the secret code of her antiquated slang.

"I can dig it completely," I said, feeling a bit idiotic.

She giggled, and I guess my heart gave a little surge of delight. "You don't dig something *completely*," she explained. "You either dig it or you don't."

"I dig it," I said—and felt a boyish flush burn across my cheeks.

IN THIS WAY was I banished from the one place on earth I really wanted to be. I wasn't in a mood to go home and start making explanations to my parents, and I certainly wasn't going to hang around Oneonta like a spurned lover. The only other place I belonged was with Reggie and Marcia Fenshaw in Tunis, so I went there. The moment I began to be enfolded in their grubby, nicotine-saturated cheeriness, I realized that Mallory (or rather Gloria MacArthur) would undoubtedly be much more at ease with them than she was with me.

Even when they finally understood that I wasn't bringing back barrels of evidence and testimony, the Fenshaws insisted that my return was a signal for celebration. A vacation from "work" was announced, though I knew that, for them, this would be more a penance than a holiday. After two days of fairly nonstop revelry, they began to fidget, and, pleading exhaustion, I retired to my apartment near the ruins of Carthage.

Tunis has never outgrown its exotic reputation, and visitors expect to be able to hear the muezzin's soulful cries on the morning air or to wander in a spicy old *madina* on a sultry afternoon. They're disappointed to find themselves in a rather commonplace French city that nowadays would seem perfectly at ease on the other side of the Mediterranean looking out on the Golfe du Lion. In fact, this explains its attraction to the Fenshaws, who belong to that special breed of very, very British types who are much more at home among the French than anywhere else.

When I've been away for a while, I'm always happy to spend a couple of days poking around in the antique shops. Many are to be found under the roof of what is said to be the Dar al-Bey, which served as guest quarters for the Ottoman Regents, and many more are clustered around the Zitouna Mosque, itself now a great museum. Charming relics of the city's romantic past abound, and it doesn't much matter that they're virtually all fakes. In the better shops, the fakes themselves are centuries old, desirable and even respectable antiques in their own right.

I wrote a preliminary report on the case of Mallory Hastings for the newsletter. I took my time over it. I took my time over everything, dawdling over menus and wine lists, planning excursions, finding a gift for my mother's birthday. At last, however, my sentence of exile was up, and I boarded a plane to wing my way back to New York.

When I finally got there, I approached Mallory's industrial-park cottage with a profound sense of dread. I pounded on the dented metal door at the front, waited, then pounded some more. At last the door swung open, and Mallory reluctantly admitted me—and the secret was revealed in an instant.

Gloria MacArthur was a painter—and not of pleasant garden scenes or arrangements of fruit on Spanish shawls. It was a moment of profound awkwardness for us both. For her part, Mallory knew how much of a shock she was presenting me with, and for mine, I knew how much of our future relationship depended on the way I handled the shock.

After a moment of stunned silence, I said, "I've never seen anything like this"—a statement full of truth but not too full.

"Yeah," she said, half deflated and, I felt, half relieved.

The children of the rich learn about art, but not the way other people learn about it. The world of art belongs to the rich, the way a certain province might belong to a prince who lives far away. In the same way that ordinary people are allowed to *inhabit* that province (though it belongs to the prince), ordinary people are allowed to *look* at the art (though it belongs to the rich). Here it should be evident that by art, I don't mean "something painted" or "something sculpted." Most of what is merely painted or sculpted never becomes art, because it never belongs to the rich. Before that, it may be the very life's blood of the painters and sculptors who starve themselves and drive themselves mad to create it. Before that, it may make interesting and striking decoration for restaurants or suburban villas. Before that, it may be collected by enterprising investors in hopes that it might someday *become* art. But it isn't art until it begins to be seen in the mansions of the wealthy and in the catalogues of the great auction houses. Then it truly leaves the domain of ordinary folk and enters the domain of the rich, who assuredly know—and assuredly teach their children—how to value and care for it.

This is what I know about art. Art is treasure that hangs on our walls, sits on our tables, and stands in our hallways. And my parents take it for granted that I'll be able to differentiate a Dürer from a Schongauer, a Steen from a Terbrugghen, an Houdon from a Canova. If the Fenshaws were to have such knowledge, this would strike my parents as marvelously droll, like a legless man owning an exquisite French racing cycle.

Since I have intimate knowledge of my family's treasures, people think I'm being modest when I tell them I know absolutely nothing about art. But if they show me a piece of student work, I won't have the slightest idea whether it's art or even "good." What I will know is whether such things hang or stand in the houses of the rich—or in the museums where the rich allow their treasures to be seen. And when people understand this, they'll instantly agree with what I said in the first place, that I know absolutely nothing about art.

But my ignorance goes beyond this. I have, additionally, no idea what's being produced in the garrets, cellars, and lofts of the art world—no idea and utterly no interest. This is not something I either brag about or apologize for. It's just how I am—and how I was when I walked into Mallory's studio.

Beyond the fact that nothing like her work has ever hung in the houses of the rich, I had no idea what I was looking at, and I told her so. To me, in my innocence, it was simply an abomination—a nauseous mess, an insolent defiance of taste, artistry, and craft. It might have been done by an ape or a lunatic or a pervert.

"Is this," I began feebly, "the sort of thing artists were doing when you—when you were . . . ?"

"When I was alive as Gloria MacArthur? Yes. Not every artist, of course. This was . . . the school of New York, you might say."

"And were you successful?"

She made a face. "I was only starting. I was . . . young." The admission seemed to stick in her throat.

I walked around, taking a polite interest. There were just four canvases in work at this point—all quite huge. She'd had only a week. I say they were "in work," but I had no real way of telling whether they were in work or finished. They reminded me of the rags painters use to clean their brushes, except on a giant scale. That anyone could be *driven* to such work struck me as profoundly pathetic.

Having nothing to say, I walked round and round the four of them groping for any plausible word of praise I could bring forth. I felt sure that adjectives like *colorful* and *different* and *interesting* would be received as merely patronizing. Finally I just told the truth and admitted I had no idea what I was looking at.

"I wouldn't expect you to," she snapped—but at the same time I had the feeling she was secretly pleased.

"Can you explain what you're trying to achieve?"

"Achieve? What are you talking about? They're *paintings*."

Clearly the word *painting* had a different meaning for the school of New York than it has for me.

She said, "Don't you have *anything* like this now?"

"Perhaps we do, Mallory. I wouldn't know. I know absolutely nothing about art."

Out of all the hundreds of statements I'd made to her, this was the first one she could swallow without a moment's hesitation.

14

TO PRESERVE its bohemian ambience, Mallory had outfitted her studio with a few sticks of furniture from something she called "the Sally." There was a high stool, a straight-backed chair, and a wobbly table covered with brushes, rags, and tubes of paint, but nothing like any traditional easels, which I gathered were only for sissies and wouldn't have accommodated her enormous canvases anyway. In a corner at the back there was a mattress and some pillows on the floor—"just for naps and things," as Mallory was still spending her nights at the condominium.

One of the rags on the table seemed familiar. I picked it up and turned it around in my hands till it came to me that it had been torn from the dress she'd worn home from the hospital. I put it back where it belonged and took notice of her work clothes for the first time—dungarees and a heavy, dark sweater. With her pale hair and pale face, she looked like a shipwreck survivor picked up from the North Sea.

We sat, I on the chair, she on the stool.

"I don't need much down here," she said, explaining the absence of amenities, "since I decided to keep the apartment for the time being."

I told her I thought that was wise, then, hearing myself, suddenly felt middle-aged and stuffy. "Let's go out and get some lunch."

"I don't eat lunch."

"Then some coffee."

"I've got gallons in a thermos."

She slid off her stool and sixty seconds later returned with two steaming mugs. It was like nothing I'd ever tasted, and Mallory said, "I hope you like chicory. It wasn't easy finding any in this fucking town."

"It's an experience," I told her. "Rather like what I'd expect asphalt to taste like if you heated it up."

She laughed and slid off her stool again. This time she returned with a bottle of bourbon. "This'll help," she said, adding a dollop to each mug. "Or at least it'll cut it."

It did that. We sipped, waited.

Finally I said, "You know I want to ask you some questions."

"Go ahead, ask."

"What year was Gloria MacArthur born?"

"Nineteen twenty-two," she replied promptly.

"A.D.?"

"Of course A.D. Do you think I painted at the court of Cleopatra?"

"Don't get huffy. I've talked to Nefertiti's hairdresser."

"What do you mean by that?"

"I mean I've talked to a woman who believes she's the reincarnation of Nefertiti's hairdresser."

She glared at me. "And you're putting me in with her?"

"Why? Do you automatically assume she's deluded?"

After pondering that for a moment, she said, "I suppose I'd better not. But do you really believe her?"

"Should I believe *you*?"

"Yes. But that's different. I'm not claiming to be Madame Pompadour's manicurist or anything like that."

"You mean I should believe you because you're not claiming to be Somebody, with a capital S."

"That's right."

"But what if you'd lived a little longer and gotten married to a Somebody—or become a Somebody in your own right. Would you expect me to scoff at you then?"

She gave that some thought. "I guess I wouldn't be surprised if you scoffed."

"Nefertiti's hairdresser isn't surprised when people scoff at her either."

This silenced her for a bit. Then she looked up and said, "But in spite of all this talk, you don't actually believe she's Nefertiti's hairdresser, do you? Admit it."

"No, I don't believe it. But that's not because she claims a famous connection. *Someone* was Nefertiti's hairdresser, after all. William Shakespeare had a housekeeper. Marie Antoinette had a manicurist. Napoleon had a valet. These were all perfectly ordinary, *real* people who were born, lived, ate, slept, worked, and one day died. Is there some reason why they should be barred from reincarnation, if such a thing exists? Should being someone famous or knowing someone famous blackball a person from the same process that put Gloria MacArthur in the body of Mallory Hastings?"

"Then why didn't you believe this woman?"

"Because she couldn't give me a credible description of the tools and materials hairdressers used in Nefertiti's time. Because she was completely up to date on who was sleeping with whom but had no idea what anybody ate for breakfast."

"Oh. I see. Yes." She sat there for a moment looking dazed. Then: "I remember once we had chicken *necks*."

"Chicken necks?"

"We were *poor*."

"This was when you were growing up?"

"Yeah."

"Where was this?"

"In Cleveland."

"Do you remember the address?"

She shook her head vaguely.

"You don't remember it?"

"I don't *want* to remember it."

"Why, Mallory?"

She winced. "I can't stand being called Mallory. What kind of name is that, anyway?"

"I don't know. At a guess, I'd say it's derived from the French *malheureux*, meaning unfortunate or unhappy."

"What could be better? It sounds like it came from one of

the knights of the fucking Round Table—Sir Mallory the Miserable."

I held out my mug, and she supplied me with a slug of bourbon.

"Did you like the name Gloria?"

She shrugged. "To tell the truth, I thought it was vulgar. Common. I don't know why. It was good enough for the Vanderbilts. Maybe I thought it was vulgar and common because *I* was vulgar and common."

It was beginning to look as if there was a cliff to fall over no matter which way I turned. "Did you have any younger brothers and sisters?"

She gave me a suspicious look. "Why do you want to know that?"

"It's not inconceivable that they might still be alive. If they were born in the 1930s, they'd only . . ." My train of thought was interrupted by a heavy ceramic mug whizzing past my right ear at fifty miles an hour and smashing on the wall behind me.

"They're *dead*!" She popped off the stool and lunged at the bourbon bottle in a way I didn't like. I grabbed it myself and twisted it out of her hands. She turned to me with bloody murder in her eyes.

"*You* killed them, you fucking cocksucker!"

As I stood there with my mouth hanging open, she started to look around for something else to throw.

"I didn't kill them," I said firmly. "I didn't kill *anybody*. I've *never* killed anybody."

"You killed them, you fucking—" She paused, speechless, then made a rapid sign, snapping her fingers together in front of her eyes, then flicking them away. "That's you," she said darkly.

"What does it mean?"

"That's what you are."

"Yes, but what does the sign *mean*?"

This question seemed to interest her, to calm her slightly. She repeated the sign thoughtfully. "It means . . . blind."

"Blind?"

"No, that's not right. Blind is this." She crooked two fingers in front of her eyes and then pulled them down as if dragging her eyelids closed. "This"—she repeated the gesture of snapping her fingers together in front of her eyes and then flicking them away—"this is a kind of shorthand or code word. It means . . . someone who's thrown sight away. Someone who refuses to see."

"I don't understand."

"It's code. Even other people who knew sign weren't supposed to understand."

"What do you mean? What 'other people who knew sign'?"

"People like you, if you happened to know sign. People who could hear normally but still knew sign for one reason or another. We could talk about . . . we could talk about people like you and only we would know who we meant."

"But who are 'people like me,' Mallory?—or Gloria, or whatever you like. Who are 'people like me'?"

She said, "People like you are murderers, Jason," but her rage was spent. "Give me the bottle."

I gave her the bottle. She took a swig, then handed it back. I took a swig myself, my own mug having gone flying during our brief wrestling match.

She got back up on her stool. I sat down.

"How am I supposed to spend the rest of my life surrounded by murderers, Jason? Murderers with beautiful white teeth and pretty clothes and nice manners and college degrees."

I gave that a minute's thought. "Maybe when I understand what you're talking about, I'll have some suggestions."

She smiled faintly and let it go.

Reached out for the bottle.

15

"I GOT INTO the art scene in New York as a model," Mallory said. "I was eighteen and I was hot stuff, baby."

We'd cleared some ground. Much as she disliked the name, she agreed it didn't make any long-term sense to call herself anything but Mallory. She wouldn't discuss her childhood, but admitted she'd lost her hearing at the age of four or five during a bout of scarlet fever.

I asked her how she learned the slang I'd heard her use. She said she didn't understand the question.

"Did you learn the word *fink* in sign language?"

"No," she said with a laugh.

"Then how do you know it now?"

She had to think about that. "I picked up slang by lip-reading," she said finally. "I wouldn't have known how to sign it, except by spelling it. Nobody said *fink* in sign, or if they did, I didn't know it. Nobody said *dig* in sign—not in the slang sense, anyway. Or maybe they did. It was two separate groups I hung out with, deaf-mutes in one group and artists in the other. Fucking Jackson Pollock didn't know any sign, that's for sure."

"Jackson Pollock was one of the artists you posed for?"

"Yeah. It was me in *The Moon-Woman*, a pretty well known painting in the early forties. That was before he swore off figurative work."

She fell silent, dreams of the past drifting across the surface of her eyes.

"Tell me more," I said after a while.

She shook her head, not in refusal but in recognition of the hopelessness of getting it all in. But then she went on. "It's funny, it looks different now, now that it's all over and locked up there in the past."

"Different how?"

"We didn't see it this clearly at the time, but the whole thing was all about these ten or twelve guys. They were the Club—I mean literally they called it the Club—and they had the *word*, y'see, and nobody else." She paused, chuckling at the memory of it. "There was Pollock and Bob Motherwell and Willem DeKooning and Mark Rothko, guys like that. You had to be one of those guys to belong to the Club, and of course you had to swear off figurative painting forever. You could have the word and swear off figurative painting, but if you didn't belong to the Club, then you were just derivative, a copycat."

"I don't understand."

"What I mean is, you could paint just like the guys in the

Club, but if you weren't actually *in* the Club—for example, if you were a woman—then it didn't count. You were just derivative."

"I'm afraid I still don't get it."

She took a minute to think how to get past my thickheadedness. "Look, the guys in the Club could all paint like each other, and that was okay. It was more than okay. To belong to the Club, you *had* to paint like the guys in the Club. But if a woman painted like them, she wasn't invited to join the Club, because she was just playing 'monkey see, monkey do.'"

"Why is that, Mallory?"

"Because only *men* know how to paint, Jason. Don't you know that, for God's sake?"

It was clear enough she was being sarcastic, but just at that moment I couldn't think of an exception to her rule. She waited half a minute, then went on.

"I don't suppose you ever heard of Lee Krasner."

I admitted I didn't.

"I met her just a few months after I arrived in New York. I guess she was about fifteen years older than me. Anyway, she'd just spent three years studying with Hans Hofmann, one of the charter members of the Club. She told me he once stood in front of one of her paintings for ten minutes, staring at it and shaking his head. Finally she said, 'Why, what's wrong?' and he said, 'There's nothing wrong. This is so good I could almost believe it was painted by a man.' He honestly thought he was paying her a terrific compliment, as if he expected her to say, 'Why, I'm sure it's *very* chivalrous of you to say that, Mr. Hofmann!'"

I had the feeling I was treading deep water here. Finally I

asked when she'd started painting herself.

"Oh shit," she said, taking another swig of bourbon. "It was all true of me—all 'monkey see, monkey do.' I was no painter. These guys had all *studied*, you know—the Art Students League, the American Artists' School, the National Academy of Design, places like that. These were professionals. I was just a fucking 'primitive.' I didn't know anything, but I watched and I learned the moves." With her head tilted to one side, she peered at me and said, "You know?"

"No," I confessed, "I don't know."

"This is all absolute horseshit," she said, gaily waving the bottle at the collection of paintings around us. "Trust me, it is," she added, as if anticipating some dissent from me.

"Then why did you paint it?"

"I was lonesome," she said simply.

I spent some time looking at it in the growing twilight. By some unknown magic, it was beginning to make a sort of sense to me. "You really think it's horseshit?"

She shrugged. "It has its moments, but they're scattered around too much to be of any use. That's what Abstract Expressionism was all about. Getting all those moments together and hitting you right in the middle of the forehead with them all at once. Some of those paintings had moments that'd knock you fucking down."

As I watched, astonished, tears filled her eyes, spilled over, and coursed down her cheeks, carving white valleys in the dust. Unlike any woman I've ever known, she didn't seem the least self-conscious or apologetic about it. She just let them flow.

After a while we had another drink.

Then, after another while, we agreed we were getting sore

sitting on those goddamned hard chairs. The mattress was there in the corner, and we didn't think anything of transferring our tortured bones to it—didn't think anything of it or mean anything by it. Mallory was in the middle of a story about her and another painter I'd never heard of.

To be blunt about it, she slept with them all. She figured this was bound to bother "a prissy-assed character" like me. I told her I could always cover my ears if it got to be too much for me.

We were getting pretty drunk.

We went on handing the bottle back and forth.

It wasn't very comfortable just sitting on the mattress. Before long, without thinking about it or meaning anything by it, we were stretched out with both our heads on her one pillow. But since there was just that one pillow, it was eventually more comfortable for us both for me to slide my arm under her shoulders.

And so on.

I woke up in the middle of the night, got dressed, and used a sketch pad to write a note saying some things I was glad to say to her and telling her I'd be in touch in a day or two.

PART TWO

FOUND

It is much easier to dig one large grave than to dig many small ones.

1 **6**

IN MY NOTE I didn't try to explain why I had to leave—or even that I did have to leave. I can't imagine how I could have.

At some point during that long, boozy evening, it all became clear to me—but not in a dazzling flash that had to be acknowledged and dealt with right away. It was rather more like a dull, echoing thud, almost a groan, that could be ignored for the time being, because, after all, it wasn't going to go away.

No, it certainly wasn't going to go away.

I had to go home. Home was where I had to be in order to figure out what to do next. I needed a place where someone would cook me things to eat without my asking for them or deciding what they should be. I needed a place where someone would open the drapes in my room in the morning and close them at night while I sat there slack-jawed, staring into the middle distance.

It took me a day and two nights to come up with a solution. It was a solution that seemed almost ridiculous, though it did (or might do) what it had to do, and I could ask for no more than that. After breakfast I invaded Mother's study, interrupting the writing of one of the dozens of charmingly intelligent letters she seemed to produce every day.

She looked up and with all the noblesse oblige of a royal instantly gave me her full attention.

"If I'm not mistaken, we own a school," I stated, knowing she would understand this shorthand, which meant that there was a school singularly in our debt owing to our generous contributions.

"Yes," she said, "a very swank little establishment for young ladies. Somewhere north of the Catskills." Bless her, she didn't add (as many a mother would), "Why do you want to know?"

"I need an extraordinary favor there. I need to borrow a class for an afternoon."

This was not shorthand, so she had to ask what I meant by borrowing a class. After I explained, she said, "I can't imagine why you'd want to do such a thing, but I'm not the person who needs to be persuaded."

Taking a sheet of notepaper from a drawer, she jotted down the name and number of that person, and that was that.

I phoned and spoke to the director, a Dr. Alwyn Reese. Like Mother, she couldn't imagine why I wanted to do such a thing. This wasn't resistance. We both knew there was practically no request from the Tull family that would have been denied, provided it wasn't manifestly illegal or immoral. She was rather in the position of a parish priest receiving a request from an archbishop fresh from a personal audience with the pope. All the same, she wanted to understand and deserved to understand.

I explained, knowing how bizarre it must sound and knowing that the entire explanation would have to be repeated at least twice more.

She listened, she paused, she thought. At last she said that Miss Crenevant's class would be the best for my purpose. Miss Crenevant taught a world history class for seniors—seventeen- and eighteen-year-olds. Dr. Reese said she'd have Miss Crenevant call me, unless I wanted to have her dragged out of class while I waited. I said it would be fine if she called at her convenience.

She called during the luncheon break.

"I'm not sure I understand what you want," Miss Crenevant said. "Dr. Reese explained, but I'm not sure I have it right."

When I asked her what she was covering in her course, she said it was the period between the birth of Christ and the so-called Great War that broke out in Europe when the heir to the Austrian throne was assassinated in Sarajevo.

"That's fine," I said. "In fact, it couldn't be better for my purpose," which I then explained again.

She listened, pondered. "It will be a good exercise for them," she said at last, meaning her students, of course.

"That's what I thought," I told her modestly. "Useful to me and a good opportunity for them to use what they've learned."

"We could actually do it tomorrow afternoon, if that's not too soon for you."

"Tomorrow afternoon will be perfect," I told her.

She thought for a moment. "Will you want me to set it up? To explain to the girls what you want from them?"

"No, I think I'd better do that."

She thought some more.

"I don't suppose you've ever been a classroom teacher."

"No, never."

"Then I feel I should warn you that girls of this age and social class—all very bright, very rich, and very spoiled— can be a handful, even for a veteran."

"Yes, I have some dim recollections of that kind from my own school days."

She replied with a silence that said I didn't know what the hell I was talking about, and she was doubtless right. I didn't think it wise to explain that it would actually help if her girls focused on the possibility of humiliating me. It would distract them from the possibility of humiliating Mallory, for whose benefit the enterprise was being mounted.

We arranged that Mallory and I would be escorted to the classroom by one of the girls, who would meet us at the school entrance between one and one-fifteen.

Having been ditched and ignored for two and a half days, Mallory was predictably rather chilly when I finally reached her at her condominium apartment that night.

"I'm not going to apologize," I told her, "because I've been working on your behalf, and I had to leave to do it."

"Working how?" she wanted to know.

"I can't explain. I'll have to show you. Will you come with me somewhere tomorrow?"

"Where?"

"If I tell you that, you'll just ask why."

"Why shouldn't I ask why?"

"Because it's something I have to show you. I'm not going to answer questions about it. Either you trust me or you don't."

"I trust you, but that doesn't mean I can't be curious."

"You can be curious all you want. At one o'clock you'll know."

"Okay."

"Where shall I pick you up, at the apartment or the studio?"

"The studio. At one o'clock?"

"No, at noon sharp. I'll tell you this much. You'll probably feel more comfortable if you're wearing something other than your painting clothes."

"You mean like a dress."

"Like a dress, yes."

"Am I supposed to impress someone?"

"No, just the opposite. Something casual and inconspicuous will do fine."

She grunted unenthusiastically.

"Noon," I repeated.

"I heard you," she snapped, and broke off the connection with a bang.

1 7

A GOOD TEN MILES from the distractions and temptations of the nearest village, the Gramercy Park Academy for Girls stood in the center of an immense walled park as bright and cheery as a prison yard. The school itself, at the end of a suitably impressive drive, was an absurd caricature, someone's idea of a stately gothic pile, as conceived, perhaps, by some dour railroad magnate in the age of Queen Victoria. Naturally it did not in fact date from that era. It was a modern horror, fashioned deliberately to overwhelm and oppress the minds of students unfortunate enough to be incarcerated there, with massive walls of gray stone streaked with moss, and tall, cramped windows admitting only enough light to allow the contemplation of one's sins or the merciful shortness of life.

Mallory and I arrived as we had traveled, in an uncomfortable silence.

On picking her up at the studio, I'd said something witty like, "You look nice," which was certainly true enough. She looked, I suppose, like a young woman applying for a job as a junior legal secretary.

She said, in a kind of savage murmur, "Mallory has exquisite taste."

The conversational tone for the journey had been set.

When she finally caught sight of the school, she said, "Are you committing me to a lunatic asylum?"

I said, "It's a school."

"What are we doing at a school?"

"Learning," I replied neatly, pulling into a parking space by the entrance.

As promised, one of the girls was waiting for us inside the cathedral-like entrance, a stout, businesslike youngster in a navy blue outfit that could only be a school uniform.

"Mr. Tull?" she said to me, darting a look at Mallory.

I told her that was right and glanced at my watch. It was 1:05.

"My name is Ava," the greeter announced. Good manners dictated a handshake and an introduction to Mallory, who said, "How do you do?" as if she'd been at it all her life.

The classroom was suitably dim, dank, and high-ceilinged.

Miss Crenevant looked like she might be Ava's mother. She was tall and rather muscular, dressed in a mannish suit, with a jowly, rectangular face, thick glasses, and russet hair in an unattractive pageboy cut. She shook our hands solemnly, as if welcoming us to a memorial service, then turned to present us to the girls, who were staring at Mallory, evidently struck by her icy beauty and sophisticated manner.

"I thought you might want these," she said, indicating two high stools she'd arranged at the front of the class.

"Yes, that's fine," I said, awkwardly leading the way.

Mallory sat down, crossed her legs precisely, and looked around with an air of detachment, establishing that none of this had anything to do with her.

I sent my eyes round the class, and the girls—fifteen or eighteen in all— switched their gaze from her to me. We were ready to begin.

"I want to start by thanking you for your time," I said and gave them a moment to snicker at this rather silly statement, since we all knew they'd had no say in the matter. "Believe it or not," I went on, "you're going to do something important in this room today, for this person here, Mallory Hastings."

Mallory shot me a perplexed, half-angry look.

"Miss Hastings," I went on, "recently had an accident in her automobile that—without going into details—caused her to suffer an unusual form of amnesia."

There was no doubt I had their attention now.

"I'm sure you know what amnesia is and what its usual effects are. The amnesiac may be missing his name, his address, even his occupation, but he hasn't forgotten how to read and speak the language he grew up with. He hasn't forgotten how to drive a car. He hasn't forgotten what money is or what it can buy. He hasn't forgotten that he's a citizen of a certain country with a certain history, a certain political structure, and so on. Yet he may not recognize either his parents or his wife and children.

"Some of this is true of Miss Hastings—and some of it isn't. There are some very fundamental things that exist in your heads that are missing in hers. These are things you take for granted, that you hardly think about at all, and that may actually seem to you quite inconsequential—almost not worth bothering about. But I'm going to ask you to dig them out of your heads for the benefit of Miss Hastings here today."

The girls exchanged bemused glances.

Ava's hand shot into the air, and I gave her a nod.

"Why don't you just tell her what she wants to know?"

"Because it isn't something she 'wants to know.' She doesn't even know it's missing."

"Even so, why not just tell her?"

"Because she probably wouldn't believe me."

This announcement produced a minor sensation. I was careful not to notice what effect it produced in Mallory.

"We know something she wouldn't believe?" This question came from the back, from a rather exotic-looking girl with a dusky, oval face and wide, dark eyes.

"May I ask your name?"

"My name is Etta."

"Thank you. I didn't exactly say you know something she wouldn't believe. What I was getting at is that she wouldn't believe it if it came from me. If it comes from you, I'm sure she'll believe it. That's exactly why we're here."

Another hand shot up, this one belonging to an elfin creature with sandy hair and freckles who announced herself as Nanette.

"Why wouldn't she believe it if it came from you?" Nanette wanted to know.

"Miss Hastings would expect anything I say to be biased. But she would have no reason to expect that of you."

Another girl raised a hand, or rather shyly turned up a palm. This was Sylvia, a child with a narrow, foxy face and wide, round glasses.

She said, "May I ask why Miss Hastings would expect anything you say to be biased?"

"Sylvia!" Miss Crenevant hissed.

"No, that's all right," I assured her. "Let's see what Miss Hastings has to say about this." I turned pointedly to Mallory. "Have I painted an accurate picture here? Would you tend to be suspicious of anything I might tell you?"

"Yes!" She was clearly steaming, ready to support any accusation I might make against myself on her behalf.

"Do you care to explain why?"

She shifted the full power of her glare onto me. "Because you're a liar. A liar and a—" I suspect it was on the tip of her tongue to call me a murderer, but, thankfully, she drew back from that.

"So," I said. "But you don't suspect these girls of being liars."

Mallory studied them, face by face. Finally she said, "I don't know what they are."

"They're ordinary high school students," I told her, fudging a bit on the "ordinary" part. The girls themselves remained still, perhaps sensing that this was not the time to assert their specialness. "You were a high school student once yourself, weren't you?"

"Yes."

"That didn't automatically make you a liar, did it?"

"No."

"I can't think why these students would be liars either. They haven't been coached. They don't have the slightest idea why we're here."

"Neither do I," Mallory snapped.

"I know. We'll remedy that soon enough." The statement came out in a more portentous style than I intended, but there was no way to call it back. The moment of truth had arrived for me, but I had no plan for it. I'd hoped vaguely that the circumstances would provide some inspiration, but there were no sparks as yet. There was nothing to do but take a leap.

"A couple of minutes ago I recited a list of things we all expect to find in our heads when we wake up in the morning. We may not remember a specific telephone number, but we haven't forgotten how to use a telephone. We may not remember a friend's exact age, but we haven't forgotten what he looks like. We may not remember the capitol of Wyoming, but we haven't forgotten the shape of the continent we're living on. We may not remember where the car's parked, but we haven't forgotten what it looks like. We may not remember the dates of the Peloponnesian War, but we haven't forgotten the general sequence of events that got us from ancient times to the present. But this last thing is exactly what Miss Hastings has forgotten and what I'd like you to reconstruct for her."

Their eyes widened in alarm.

"Miss Crenevant tells me that what you've been reviewing here is the period between the birth of Christ and the Great War. Is that right?"

They nodded warily, as if they thought anything more exuberant might encourage me to spring a surprise quiz on them.

"What did the combatants in the Great War think it was all about? Can you tell me that?"

The girls shifted uneasily in their seats.

Miss Crenevant stepped in to give them a hint. "You remember we discussed why, at the time, the war was so difficult for the combatants to understand or explain, even to each other."

After a moment the foxy-faced Sylvia shot her hand up into the air and began waggling it furiously.

"Go ahead, Sylvia," I said, taking charge.

"They weren't looking far enough back," she said. "They didn't see that this was just the final battle in a war that had been going on for almost two thousand years."

"A covert, undeclared war," Miss Crenevant added, setting the record straight. "Carried on without guns and bombs. By other means."

I nodded. "I learned the same thing when I was in school—and so did Miss Hastings, of course, though she has utterly no memory of it now. She's in the same position as the combatants in the Great War. That's what we're here to correct today. Who were the perpetrators of this covert two-thousand-year-old war?"

The girls' eyes widened in surprise. Surely it wasn't going to be *this* easy! This was kindergarten stuff. A dozen voices supplied the answer:

"The Jews!"

I sensed, rather than saw, Mallory stiffen at my side.

"And who was the war being waged against?"

"Us!"

"What was the background of the war? Why were the Jews waging war on us?"

This was a bit more challenging. After a moment's silence, Miss Crenevant fastened her eyes on the dark beauty known as Etta and reminded her that she had written her mid-term paper on this very subject. Even so, it took Etta a few seconds to connect her paper to my question. When she finally had it, it came out almost by rote.

"The Aryan race in its European homeland represented the high-water mark of human evolution. Natural selection had made the Aryans the cream, the elite. The rest, for the most part, were just savages at one stage or another. They didn't know or care that one race had stepped ahead on the evolutionary scale—except for the Jews. The Jews knew and cared, and they wanted to supplant the Aryans as the elite of the human race. Or if they couldn't supplant them, they wanted to control them—manipulate them covertly. This is the background you need to have in order to understand the whole story."

"Okay," I said. "But this period in history you're studying begins with the birth of Christ. Why there? What did Christ have to do with it?"

"He was a Jew," someone noted.

"Certainly, but why begin with this particular Jew? Why not with Moses?"

After a bit of dithering, Sylvia took a stab at it. "At the time when Christ died, the Jews were not a tremendous force in the world."

"Yes, that's true, but why does it matter?"

"Because Christianity opened up the world to Jewish ideas."

"You'll have to expand on that a little bit," I told her. "It sounds almost like a contradiction."

"The original followers of Jesus were Jews living in Jerusalem. They thought of Jesus as one of themselves (which he was, of course), with a message for the Jewish people. Christianity, to the extent that it existed as a separate thing, was a Jewish religion, originally."

"Go on."

"It was Paul who thought of exporting it to the Roman world. But to do that, he had to . . . he had to—what's the word I want?—he had to revamp it. The religion as it was being practiced in Jerusalem would have been too Jewish for Roman tastes. Paul had to spice it up with ideas Romans would understand and accept. Like the idea of Jesus being offered up as a sacrifice for mankind. The Jews would never have gone for an idea like that."

"You seem to know a lot about it."

"I read a book," Sylvia announced grandly.

"Go on, please."

"Well, as I say, Paul had to spice it up with Roman ideas, but it was still basically a bunch of Jewish concepts. Like the idea of there being just one God, instead of all the pagan gods the Romans had around, like Jupiter and Venus and so on."

"Okay. And is this what you mean when you say that Christianity opened up the world to Jewish ideas?"

"Yeah, that's it. Christianity made the Roman world a more comfortable place for the Jews, because the Romans now worshiped the God of the Jews."

"How comfortable was it for them? For example, did the Roman Empire ever have a Jewish emperor?"

That got a laugh.

"They weren't *that* comfortable," someone said.

"But then the Roman Empire fell," Natalie said with an air of triumph, as if this might be the chief item in her historical treasury. "That was in 476."

"Then what?" I prompted.

"The Dark Ages," someone muttered.

"I *hate* the Dark Ages," said Sylvia.

"I hate the *Middle Ages*," said Nanette.

I was glad to see they were beginning to relax.

Ava said, "During the Dark Ages and Middle Ages, that was when the Jews really began to consolidate their power in European culture. At least that's what I'd say."

"What was going on in this period?"

Hands shot into the air and I pointed to an overweight child with long, stringy dark hair, who introduced herself as Gilda. "Most of what went on in this period," she said, "was a reaction to the presence of the Jews in Europe."

"But what *was* going on?"

The girls traded glances and agreed on an answer: *nothing*.

"It was a period of stagnation on all fronts," Gilda said flatly.

"Okay. Nothing was going on in this period, and this was a reaction to the presence of the Jews. Is that what you're saying?"

After a blank moment, Miss Crenevant gave them a hint: "We studied this just before the mid-winter break."

Nanette's hand shot into the air, and I nodded.

"The Jews controlled the banking," she said. "Or was this too early for banking? I guess it really doesn't matter. What I mean is, they *acted* as the bankers. They controlled the money. I mean, like when two kings wanted to go to war with each other, both of them had to borrow money from the Jews."

"They *wanted* to borrow money from the Jews," Sylvia emended. "They didn't want to risk using their own."

"But what does this have to do with nothing happening?" I asked.

Sylvia shrugged. "I guess the Jews didn't *want* anything to happen. I mean, they controlled the money, and everything was fine as far as they were concerned, so why would they want things to change?"

"Okay. But things did change anyway, eventually."

"Right," said Ava. "During the Renaissance."

"And why did things change during the Renaissance?"

A sea of waving hands sprang up, signaling that they had this one down pat. I pointed to a girl who hadn't spoken yet, a towheaded child who would be very pretty when her braces came off. She said, "People rediscovered a source of ideas that predated the Jews. They went back to ideas that had been flourishing in classical times, before the Jews began to push their way into Europe. The Renaissance began when the people of Europe reconnected with their Aryan past."

"Literature, the arts, scholarship, and science flourished," Ava chirped.

"Galileo," someone volunteered.

"The Reformation."

"The printing press."

They'd found a solid bit of ground, and I let them go on exploring it.

"Michelangelo."

"Queen Elizabeth."

"Shakespeare!"

Finally Nanette seemed to deliver the capper. "It was a period of global exploration and commercial expansion."

I nodded professorially, then stopped them in their tracks by observing that the Jews must have been pretty unhappy about all this.

"Not at all," Miss Crenevant snapped, unwilling to let her pupils find their own way through this challenge. "Remember *The Merchant of Venice*, girls. The excitement of exploration and of building new trade routes appealed to great-hearted men like Antonio. But the free-spirited Aryan adventurers of the era lived at the sufferance of Jewish backers who cared for nothing but their percentage. All the Jews wanted was their pound of flesh—and they usually got it. This is the obvious subtext of the play. But that," she added portentously, "was only half of it."

She looked around the room hopefully but was rewarded by blank stares. Finally she relented and gave them a sentence they knew how to complete. "The process of exploration in Africa, the New World, and the Pacific Rim also brought them into contact with . . ."

"The mongrel races!" the girls chorused triumphantly.

Mallory slid off her stool and headed unsteadily for the door.

"We'll take a short break," I said over my shoulder as I went after her.

She was huddled in a corner, back firmly against a wall, arms crossed protectively across her chest.

"I want to go home," she whimpered.

"Soon," I said. "Not yet."

"I *know* all this. I *guessed* all this."

"That's not true. You couldn't have."

"I mean . . . I knew it had to be *something* like this."

I shook my head. "You don't know *anything* yet."

"I know it all."

"You *don't* know it all. You couldn't possibly. What's still to come is beyond anything you could imagine."

She looked around bleakly. "I don't need it."

"You *do* need it. You've got to have it."

"Please," she whispered.

"No. This is something you've got to do. Something *we've* got to do."

She let her shoulders slump in defeat, and I took her arm to lead her back. At the door she stopped and said, "At least let me sit at the back."

"What?"

"Tell Miss What's-her-name to clear a row for me at the back so I don't have to sit there like Exhibit A. I'll be able to hear just as well from back there."

1 8

WHEN THE GIRLS were reseated the way Mallory wanted them and had settled down, I said, "Okay, when we broke off, we'd just heard about the mongrel races. What exactly were these?"

This was an easy one, and Gilda of the stringy dark hair stuck up her hand first. "These were the nonevolved races. There were *hordes* of these not-quite-human types who were black and yellow and brown and red—and every mixture."

"And what's their significance in this story we're developing here?"

That was not so easy, and they spent a couple of minutes discussing it in whispers. Finally, Miss Crenevant had to be called in to affirm their judgment, which Ava delivered.

"Christianity first opened the Aryan world to the Jews.

Now it opened the Aryan world to these even less evolved races."

"How did Christianity do that?"

Ava shrugged. "By sending them missionaries. By making them Christians. As Christians themselves, the Aryans then had to accept them as equals. According to Christianity, God loved everyone equally."

"Okay, but I'm getting lost here," I said. "According to what you've told me, the Jews had been waging an undeclared war against the Aryans since the time of Christ. Christianity had brought them inside the Aryan world, where they could manipulate and control, but this hadn't won them the war. Now you seem to be saying that the Jews were developing a new strategy to defeat the Aryans and this new strategy somehow involved these subhuman races."

Miss Crenevant, becoming impatient with my Socratic method, stepped in to answer my implied question herself. "The height of the missionary efforts of Christians came during the seventeenth, eighteen, and nineteenth centuries, and it was during this period that the Jews began to realize that there was another way to reach their objective. They couldn't overcome our natural superiority, but they could undermine it by mongrelizing us. They could bring the Aryan race down to their own level by breeding us with Jews and other mongrel races."

"And how were they going to accomplish this?"

"First of all, by promoting the idea that the mongrel races were just as good. That was the whole point of Christianizing them. If they were worthy of God, then why wouldn't they be worthy of us?"

"And then?" I asked. "What was the next step in their program?"

"Very simply, the Great War," Miss Crenevant said. "Everyone could see that this war served no rational political purpose. What they *couldn't* see—at least initially—was that it served a Jewish purpose, which was to pit the Aryan nations against each other, exhausting them morally and economically and enriching the Jews, who supplied all the combatants with arms and ammunition."

"Go on. What happened then?"

"Eventually one coalition of Aryan nations won out, but this only paused the war for a few years while the loser—the Germans, basically—recovered. Then they went at it again. But by this time, the Germans knew that the real enemy was the Jews, who had been the instigators and beneficiaries of the war from the start."

"So the war resumed," I said. "And did the combatants still not understand why they were fighting?"

Miss Crenevant reflected on this for a moment. "The two sides now had different understandings of why they were fighting. The Germans understood that the real enemy was the Jews, and the Jews were the real target of their enmity. But the Aryan nations allied against them didn't see this yet. So, in effect, the Germans were fighting two wars, one against their Aryan brothers (who called themselves the Allies) and one against the Jews."

"So what happened?"

"Finally the Germans scored a decisive victory over the Jews in a small town in Bavaria, essentially turning the tide against them. Once the Jews had been taken out of the war in this battle, the Germans were unstoppable, so much so that the Allies finally understood what had been going on."

"What do you mean by that?"

"The battle against the Jews had been a secret one for the Germans, bleeding away their resources year in and year out. But once *that* battle was over, the Allies could see the Germans growing strong again, almost immediately."

"You mean the Allies finally saw that the Germans had been fighting two wars, one of which the Allies hadn't even guessed at."

"That's right. And at that point the Allies and the Germans made peace and turned their attention to the global elimination of the Jewish plague."

"A new era had begun."

"Absolutely."

"There was a general recognition that the Christian era had in fact been a Jewish era."

"That's right. The Christian dating system was junked, and a new zero year was adopted worldwide."

"And what event marked that zero year?"

That was an easy one, of course, and Miss Crenevant let someone else answer it: "The defeat of the Jews at Dachau, that little town in Bavaria."

"So from that point on we've counted our years as years A.D.: years After Dachau. And how many—"

"What *I* don't get," growled Gilda, "is the A.D.-A.D. thing."

Miss Crenevant began to scold her for interrupting, but I interrupted Miss Crenevant to ask for an explanation.

"The years *before* A.D.. are *also* A.D.," Gilda said.

I looked at Miss Crenevant, and she coolly returned my

gaze, letting me know that if I was going to run the class, I could jolly well run it on my own.

I cleared my throat and blinked twice while assembling my recitation. "The A.D. of the Christian era stands for *anno Domini,* a Latin phrase meaning 'in the year of our Lord.' If you give the start date of the Great War as A.D. 1914, for example, this translates as 'in the year of our Lord 1914.' But if you were to give that date as 1914 A.D., this would translate as '1914 in the year of our Lord,' which doesn't make any sense. The placement always lets you know which dates are which. A.D. 576 refers to the Christian era but 576 A.D. refers to our own. Okay?"

Gilda guessed so, but her grimace of disgust let us know what she thought of the dunces who couldn't manage the affairs of the world better than this.

"I was about to ask how many years After Dachau have passed by now."

This raised a roomful of laughs, since this was indeed kindergarten stuff.

"Two thousand and two!" they roared, celebrating what finally appeared to be a linking of "then" to "now."

A voice from the rear interrupted the celebration.

"Dachau wasn't a battle," Mallory stated through clenched teeth. "It was a concentration camp."

The girls twisted in their seats to look at her. They were plainly stunned—not by what she'd said but by the fact that she'd said anything at all.

"What's a concentration camp?" one of them asked.

"It's a collection point for people—in this case, Jews destined for extermination."

Puzzled, the girls turned to their teacher, who seemed to

share their puzzlement. "Certainly many thousands of Jews died at Dachau," she said.

"But it wasn't a battle," Mallory insisted.

"What was it?" the teacher asked.

"It was . . . it was a campaign of deliberate extermination."

Miss Crenevant frowned. "I'm afraid the distinction eludes me. Any battle is a campaign of deliberate extermination, surely. Soldiers who are shooting at each other and throwing bombs at each other aren't just doing it for fun."

"But that's just the point. The Jews at Dachau weren't soldiers, they were unarmed civilians, including women and children."

Miss Crenevant's frown was replaced by a look of frank astonishment. "I'd be fascinated," she said, "to know where you got such a bizarre idea."

"You actually don't know, do you," Mallory said, dazed. "You actually believe it was a battle."

Miss Crenevant gave her a not unkindly smile. "As much as I believe that Thermopylae or Hastings or Verdun were battles."

Mallory shrank into her seat.

① ⑨

"HOWEVER," I said, "we've still got a way to go to bring us from there to here." I looked around the room and picked a youngster at the back with frizzy blond hair and a wide, humorous mouth. She said her name was Betty.

"Well, Betty, we haven't heard from you yet. Why don't you carry us forward?"

She looked alarmed at being singled out in this way, so I lent her a hand. "The Aryan nations of the world had been at each other's throats for thirty years. Now they shared a new, common understanding of the world situation."

"Yes, they all knew that the Jews were the enemy, not each other."

"That's right. But there was a lot more to it than that. The unevolved peoples you've called the mongrel races didn't just

121

quietly disappear at the end of the Great War, did they? What had been happening to them during all the missionary centuries?"

Clearly no one had a clue what I was getting at.

"Think," I said, "about China."

"Ah-h-h-h-h-h," they said, catching up at last.

Ava allowed herself to raise a tentative hand, and I gave her an encouraging nod.

"The missionaries had been bringing more to the mongrel races than just God," she said. "They'd been bringing them improved health care and medical advances from the Aryan nations and improved agricultural techniques."

"And what was the consequence of all these gifts?"

"Their populations grew."

"Their populations *exploded*," someone amended.

Betty again: "This supported the Jewish strategy of world domination."

"How so?" I asked.

"The idea was to *overwhelm* the Aryans in mongrels."

"But how would this help the Jews? If the Aryans were overwhelmed, wouldn't the Jews be overwhelmed as well?"

The girls traded doubtful glances, and after a moment Miss Crenevant stepped in. "I think only more advanced students would be prepared to answer this question. The Jews were famously cliquish," she said. "They stuck to their own with a kind of fierce, tribal exclusivity."

"And this explains why the Jews wouldn't be overwhelmed by the expansion of the mongrel races?"

"Yes. Lacking this rabid cliquishness, the Aryans would eventually be swallowed up in the mongrel flood, but the Jews would continue to hold themselves aloof. When the

Aryans disappeared, the Jews would still be there, the only distinct race of pure blood. This would make them, by default, the master race of the world."

Mallory groaned and laid her head down on her arms on the desk in front of her. The girls pretended not to notice, but their eyes widened in dismay.

"A vicious plot," I observed reassuringly. "So what happened next? We still have a long way to go to bring us to the present."

"The Aryan Council of Nations was formed in 11 A.D.," Etta offered.

Now that familiar, solid ground had been reached at last, the class visibly relaxed.

"It would probably be more accurate," Miss Crenevant interposed, "to say that the Aryan Council of Nations was formally *recognized* in 11 A.D. In the years immediately following Dachau, not all nations were ready to acknowledge or embrace the reality of the situation."

"In the old, Christian style of reckoning, when was the Aryan Council formally recognized?" I asked.

For the answer to that, they had to go to their textbooks. "It would have been 1954," Ava declared after a bit of searching.

I said, "Tell us a bit about the Council. What was its mission?"

This was the sort of question they expected to see in their quizzes, and they began paging listlessly through their textbooks to find the answer. I interrupted to tell them I just wanted a brief summary, a thumbnail sketch. A couple of girls sighed; two or three shuffled their feet. No one cared to volunteer.

I said, "The author of the Council charter refers to the Spirit of Dachau. What did he mean by that?"

Etta shrugged her shoulders. "He meant it was necessary for the Aryan nations to be as cold as ice. Those were the words he used, 'cold as ice.'"

"And what did this mean?"

They stirred sullenly, and I realized I was on the brink of losing them. "Miss Crenevant," I said. "Maybe you can assist."

She seemed relieved to take over. "We'd always taken our natural superiority over the unevolved races for granted, much the way we do with our pets and farm animals, and this nearly led to our downfall. The author of the charter was saying it was time for Aryan peoples to suppress their natural magnanimity and do what had to be done next to safeguard the future of the human race."

"And what was that? What had to be done next?"

"The Spirit of Dachau had to be carried across the entire face of the earth."

"Meaning what, exactly?"

"That humanity had to purge itself of mongrel strains once and for all."

"Why?"

"Why? Because at the rate they were breeding, we'd soon be facing another crisis as horrendous as the one we'd just barely survived."

"How long did it take for humanity to purge itself of mongrel strains once and for all?"

"A long time."

"And how do you feel about this?"

"You mean . . . me, personally?"

"Yes, if you don't mind."

"No one feels wonderful about it," she said with a shrug. "It was necessary and, after all, not without precedent."

"What do you mean by that?"

"The story of human evolution doesn't follow the same pattern as the evolution of other creatures. When reptiles emerged from the amphibians, they didn't destroy the amphibians. When mammals emerged from the reptiles, they didn't destroy the reptiles. But the same is not true of humans. Among humans, each emerging species apparently destroyed the species from which it emerged. This explains why none of those earlier species survived to the present time. In fact, most biologists feel this accounts for the tremendous speed with which humans evolved from lower forms."

"So we Aryans were only doing what humans have done from the beginning."

"Exactly," said Miss Crenevant. "And in fact we made it all the more painful and difficult for ourselves by *refraining* from doing it for as long as we did."

"Thank you. But I'd like to return to my earlier question. How long did it take?"

"It took at least eight hundred years. So long as we knew it was being done—and systematically done—there was no need to rush. In some parts of the world the process was so gradual that there was virtually no resistance at all. It may even have taken longer than eight hundred years. No one knows exactly when the last non-Aryan disappeared."

"But in any case," I said, "this explains why, if you were to visit the bookstores and libraries of the world and assemble all the books you could locate showing photographs of people—movie stars, fashion models, musicians, workers, farmers, people at sporting events, school children, and so on—you wouldn't be able to find a single face in them that wasn't white. For more than a thousand years, there hasn't been such a face. For more than a thousand years, being human has meant being Aryan and nothing else."

"That's correct."

I held out a hand to Mallory and said, "We're done."

As she made her way to the front of the room, I thanked Miss Crenevant and the girls for their assistance. Then I asked if anyone knew how Napoleon Bonaparte had defined history. No one did.

"Napoleon said, 'History is just an agreed-upon fiction.'"

They looked at me as blankly as if I'd just said something in Greek.

"I have a question," Mallory said to them. "You all talked about the author of the Aryan Council's charter as if this was a single individual."

The girls nodded.

"Let me see if I've learned anything here today about how you put this history of yours together. I'm going to guess that the author of the charter was the man who turned the tide against the Jews. He's probably known as the Hero of Dachau."

The girls were amazed and delighted with Mallory's evident progress.

"Is his name known?" This question was greeted with giggles and tickled affirmations.

"Let's see if I can guess it," Mallory said. Even before the words *Adolf Hitler* were out of her mouth, the girls broke into congratulatory applause, coming out of their seats in a spontaneous celebration of her recovery. It was manifest that Mallory's "amnesia" had been triumphantly cured.

As we turned to leave, Miss Crenevant deftly interposed herself between us and the exit. "Dr. Reese asked if you would grant her an opportunity to extend a personal greeting to you."

"Please convey my apologies to Dr. Reese, along with my sincere thanks," I told her, "but this has been a more traumatic experience for Miss Hastings than you might be able to guess."

It was churlish of me, but we Aryans know when it's time to be cold as ice.

20

MALLORY, never predictable, seemed almost preternaturally calm as we tramped down the school's echoing hallways and out to the parking lot. She still hadn't spoken by the time we were in the car and headed back the way we came. Unable to think of anything else, I lamely told her I was sorry she'd had to go through that.

"There's no need to be sorry," she said. "Have you ever had a sliver in your hand?"

"Of course I have. I've led a sheltered life, but not *that* sheltered."

"The last thing you want is anyone digging around for it, but once it's out, all you feel is relief. You can look at this tiny splinter of wood, see it for what it is, and throw it away. I knew there was a sliver there—I've known that from the first day I woke up in the hospital as Mallory Hastings—but it was so huge I was afraid it would tear me apart if it ever came out." She watched the scenery flow past the window for a while. "Now it's out and it's gone, and I feel sort of empty—but not torn to pieces. I'm relieved to know who I am and where I am, and how I got here." After a bit she added, "But I do feel sort of empty."

I left her alone and drove on. When we connected with the highway to Oneonta, she asked me to pull over.

"This is probably a silly question," she said when we were stopped, "but I have to know the answer anyway. Are you a not-see?"

"A not-see? What's that?"

She laughed. "Not a not-see. *This* is a not-see." She repeated the sign she'd used earlier to characterize me, snapping her fingers together in front her eyes and tossing them away. "*Not-see* is a sign-language pun."

"I don't get it."

"*Not-see* equals *Nazi*—N-A-Z-I."

"I still don't get it. What's a Nazi?"

Her eyes widened in amused disbelief. "The Nazis were the collective 'heroes of Dachau.' Hitler was the leader of the Nazis—he was their saint, their *beau idéal*, their knight in shining armor."

"I see. But that still doesn't tell me what a Nazi is."

"It's short for *National Socialist*—I assume it comes from the original German."

"Okay. That part rings a bell. National Socialism was popular all over Europe for a time—but never in the U.S."

"But you still managed to murder your Jews."

"Is that the real meaning of the word *Nazi*—Jew-killer?"

"Yeah, I guess it is."

"And this is why you call me a murderer?"

She nodded.

I thought about the charge for a while, then said, "The greatest library of the ancient world, full of unique and unreplaceable manuscripts, was in Alexandria. Near the end of the fourth century, the Roman emperor Theodosius had it burned so as to rid the world of all those horrid pagan works, most of which were lost to us forever, since they existed nowhere else. Did you feel guilty about this act of barbarism when you were alive as Gloria MacArthur?"

She shook her head. "Feeling guilty isn't the issue. Certainly it isn't the issue with those little girls and their teacher. As far as they're concerned, killing millions of people was like getting rid of fleas on a pet dog—just an unpleasant but necessary chore."

There was nothing to say to that. After a minute of silence, I started the car again.

"Don't do that," she told me, and I turned it off. She continued to stare out the window on her side of the car. Finally, she said, "What happened to you people?"

"What do you mean?"

"When I was alive back in the twentieth century—back in *my* twentieth century—people imagined that a great new age was just ahead. All the work was going to be done by robots. Everybody would have personal helicopters and live like kings in a kind of gadget-filled paradise. But in fact nothing's changed. Everything's exactly the way it was two thousand years ago. What happened?"

"I wish you'd asked this question back at the Academy. Then you could have heard the 'official' answer."

"And what is that?"

"That the frantic desire for 'progress' that drove your nineteenth and twentieth centuries was a product of Jewish greed. The Jews wanted people to buy a whole set of new products every spring and then throw them away for a 'better' set in the fall. Nothing was supposed to last. Everything was designed to fall apart so it could be replaced by something 'better.' That's the answer I learned in school. That's the answer Mallory Hastings learned in school—and that you forgot during your period of unconsciousness."

She shook her head impatiently. "You're trying to have it both ways. First you tell me the Jews were behind the *lack* of progress in the Middle Ages, now you tell me they were behind the *rush* of progress in the nineteenth and twentieth centuries. Which is it?"

"It's both. Do you want to hear how Ava or Nanette would explain it?"

"I guess I can work it out on my own. But it still doesn't explain the utter stagnation of your Aryan paradise."

"Doesn't it? Think about it. We don't believe in novelty for the sake of novelty. Novelty for its own sake is a *Jewish* thing, you see. We believe in making good things to start with—things that *last*. And we believe in making them as good this year as we did last year—as good as they were in my grandfather's day and in *his* grandfather's day. The basic systems that make this automobile function haven't been improved for two thousand years because they don't *need* to be improved. We're *proud* of this, you understand. This is an *Aryan* car, not a Jewish car that starts falling apart as soon as you take it out of the showroom. This is the explanation we heard from our parents and they heard from their parents and they heard from their parents and they heard from their parents, all the way back to the signing of the Aryan Council Charter."

"I see."

"Does the explanation make sense?"

"I guess it does, if you accept all those premises about Jews and Aryans."

"Do you think the girls in Miss Crenevant's classroom question it?"

"No, I suppose not."

"Certainly not. And why should they? There's absolutely nothing wrong with this good, solid, boring Aryan automobile, after all."

"Okay. But is this true of everybody? Doesn't *anybody* question it?"

I had to give that some thought. "I think everyone questions it—but only with about one percent of their minds. We're ninety-nine percent sure that what we have is truly a wonderful Aryan paradise, as you call it. But then there's that other one percent that makes us wonder what the hell is *wrong* with us."

"Don't you ever try *answering* that question?"

"No, because maybe we couldn't stand hearing the answer. We're afraid to know what's wrong with us."

"I'd be afraid too, if I were you," Mallory said, and opened the passenger door.

"What are you doing?"

"I'm going back to Oneonta," she said, getting out. "I'll hitch a ride."

"Don't be silly."

She started to close the door, then paused, evidently

thinking of something to add. "Speaking of my being silly, do you remember your concern about my 'mother'?"

"What do you mean?"

"You didn't want to take me to New York City without getting her permission."

"Right. I remember."

"Do you know how many times she's called since I got out of the hospital? Zero times. Her one and only concern about me was the possibility that my being in the hospital might reflect badly on her. Her only concern was to get me out of there so I'd stop embarrassing her. Which I knew well enough at the time, and you didn't."

"Okay. So?"

"So you should shut up about me being silly. You're no expert."

"Okay, I take it back. I apologize. But there's no reason why you should hitch a ride to Oneonta. I'll be glad to take you there."

"Your gladness doesn't enter into it. This is something I'm doing because I want to do it. Understand?"

"I understand," I said, and she slammed the door and walked away. I considered hanging around till she got a ride. I also considered hanging around till she got a ride, and then following her northward to Oneonta to make sure she got home safely. But in the end I knew this would only infuriate her, so I turned the car around and headed back to Manhattan.

21

WHEN I WOKE the next morning after a pleasant evening with my parents, I realized I'd become a man without a plan or a purpose—something new to me (and not altogether unpleasant). For the first time in a long while, I wasn't getting ready to do something or waiting for someone else to do something. I was in a position to behave like one of the idle rich: go shopping in elegant stores for unneeded things, meet similarly idle friends for lunch or cocktails, catch a show or a concert in the evening, all of which I somewhat dutifully attended to on that day, a Wednesday.

The following morning, with no clear plan in mind, I went for a walk and ended up in a bookstore, where I wandered listlessly for an hour, fingering novels and collections of short stories, looking for escapist reading. I felt out of place and a trifle guilty, because in fact I'm not much of a reader. I was afraid some clerk would offer to assist or make a recommendation, and I'd be revealed as an ignorant philistine. At last I selected three novels, paid for them, and fled, feeling like a lapsed alcoholic sneaking out of a liquor store with a bottle under his arm.

Not caring to go back home so soon, I took my acquisitions to the Metropolitan, which is the only thing the Tulls mean when they speak of "the club." It has the odd (and probably undeserved) reputation of having been founded in ancient times to cater to an especially worldly and wicked clientele, who are certainly nowhere in evidence today. Still, it's not quite as stuffy as such establishments tend to be and is stocked with all the usual clubby amenities, though the only ones I wanted were a comfortable chair, a good light, and an occasional glass of sherry at my elbow.

I wasn't doing research. Nothing could have been further from my mind. I was making an earnest effort to amuse myself for a few hours, and the novels I'd chosen at the bookstore were presumably written for exactly this purpose. I opened one, read for half an hour, then set it aside in favor of a second—which I also read for half an hour and set aside. I picked up the third and, in a state of bemused distraction, wandered into the dining room for lunch. I pondered matters over a cocktail, spent fifteen minutes reading, then set the third book aside as well when my entree arrived.

Without intending any such thing, I'd made what was (for me) a remarkable discovery. I'd told the girls at the academy that Napoleon considered history "just an agreed-upon fiction." An hour's reading in the work of three different authors revealed an unsuspected dimension of truth in this description. It was clear that all three had studied with Miss Crenevant (or one of her clones), though there isn't a trace of historical reference in their books. All had a contemporary setting, featuring characters that could be said to be just like me. Not one of us questions the verity that the human race is exactly congruent with the Aryan race—and was "meant" to be congruent with the Aryan race from the foundation of the universe. Not one of us gives a moment's thought to the absence of "other" faces in our midst. Like me, the characters in these books travel the world, knowing with absolute assurance that the people we'll see in Tokyo or Shanghai or Johannesburg or Bombay will be as uniformly white as the people in Paris or Chicago or Sydney. For us, indeed, white is the color of people, the way yellow is the color of bananas. To see a red man in Santa Fe would be as startling as to see a lavender lion in Africa. White is the suitable color for people, as tawny yellow is for lions.

Like me, all these authors and their characters occupy a world in which the Great War is essentially the stuff of legend, as the Trojan War must have seemed in Gloria MacArthur's day. The Jews have hardly more reality for us than the dragons of the Middle Ages, and the Merchant of Venice inhabits the same fairy-tale universe as the Pied Piper of Hamelin.

We don't live in a world that is *stagnant*, as Mallory dubbed it. We live in a world that is *stable*—wonderfully stable, blessedly stable, as it *deserves* to be for the race that is the pinnacle of cosmic development.

Mallory seemed to think I should live in sackcloth and ashes because my ancestors exterminated the original inhabitants of Asia and Africa to make room for people like me. I made a mental note to ask her if Jackson Pollock lived in sackcloth and ashes because his ancestors exterminated the original inhabitants of North America to make room for people like him.

It isn't just *our* history that is an agreed-upon fiction.

When I got home, I was informed that Mother was waiting for me with a guest in her study. This wasn't food for thought, since my mother receives dozens of visitors a month, none of whom would miss a chance to pat the young master on the head. I was therefore startled to see that Mother's guest was Mallory, dressed for the city in a dark suit and white blouse. She stood up when I came in, disconcerting me further. What was she expecting? My mother cocked an eyebrow at me in amusement, needing only a millisecond to register my uncertainty. I decided that if Mallory was going to play Lady Caller, I'd have to play Gentleman Host, so I stepped forward and gave her an awkward embrace, punctuated with a peck on the cheek.

Explanations followed. Mallory had telephoned, but too late to catch me. The call had been transferred to Mother, who certainly wouldn't let such an opportunity slip by. They'd been together since eleven and had just finished lunch.

Mother said, "Mallory tells me she has a suite at the Commodore. Have you ever heard of it?"

I said I hadn't.

"That's a sort of joke," Mallory explained. "Do you know the Escorial?"

"Of course," I said. "It's a five-star establishment adjoining Grand Central Station."

"In quite ancient times there was another five-star establishment in exactly that location, known as the Commodore. I'm sure it's been gone for centuries, but at the time it was the cat's whiskers." She gave me a sardonic wink that she knew my mother couldn't catch.

"I see," I said gravely, not knowing what else to say.

"Anyway," she went on, "now that you're here, we're ready for an expedition."

"We are? What sort of expedition?"

"The same as yours—the kind you're not allowed to ask questions about."

"I see," I said again, obviously not seeing anything.

"But I can tell you this much—you'll have to wear different clothes."

"What kind of clothes?"

"The kind you won't mind getting dirty." When she saw me eyeing her own outfit, she told me we'd be stopping at her hotel so she could change.

I glanced again at my mother, who had been following the interchange with silent merriment, then turned and marched off to my room to change.

"If you're going to sulk," Mallory said when we were in the car, "I'll give you a hint about where we're going."

"I'm not sulking," I told her. "I'm brooding. There's a subtle difference."

"Is there? I didn't know that."

Mallory had changed—subtly but profoundly—in the forty hours that had passed since I last saw her. Or perhaps it would be more accurate to say that Gloria had changed.

She had in some mysterious way grown into, taken over, and fused with the body, the clothes, and the life of Mallory Hastings. This was a different person from the one I'd rescued from the hospital, perhaps the one who began to emerge during our visit to the Gramercy Park Academy for Girls.

I said, "I could see that you and Mother were getting along very nicely."

"Yes, we were. Is that what you're brooding about?"

"I think it is, yes. I'm a very possessive person, I fear."

"Are you worried that I might take Mother away?"

I said no and let it go at that. It was the opposite possibility that worried me, that Mother might take Mallory away. Since I didn't care to mention this, I asked her what hint she was prepared to offer about our expedition.

"You told me a story about a little boy who remembered hiding something behind a loose brick in a house he'd lived in during a previous life."

"That's right," I told her. "Eddie Tucker."

"I want to take you to my own 'loose brick.'"

I drove for a bit as I pondered this, then said, "I hope you're not serious."

"Why?"

"After two thousand years? Think about it. The Empire State Building has been razed and rebuilt from the original plans not once but three times since you saw it as Gloria MacArthur."

She was unfazed. "Two thousand years ago I put something down in a certain place. Today I'll go and pick it up, right where I left it."

"Will you tell me what it is?"

"No. Why?"

"So that when you find it . . ."

She grimaced. "So I can't just pick up something at random and say, 'This is it.'"

"I know you wouldn't do that. I want you to tell me what it is so that when you find it, I can testify that it was what you said it would be."

She surprised me by bursting into laughter. "I'd forgotten about all that. You still want to make your 'case.' What did you call it? The Golden Case?"

"It's just something I owe the Fenshaws."

"I tell you what," Mallory said. "I'll write it down on a piece of hotel stationery and seal it in an envelope, then you can hang onto it if you promise not to peek."

"Of course I won't peek," I snapped, raising another laugh.

2 2

I WAITED IN the car for her to go up and change, and when she returned twenty minutes later, I said, "Where are we going, the Himalayas?" Along with her dungarees (which she had taught me to call jeans), she was wearing a heavy-looking backpack and was carrying another one, evidently for me. She slung them both in the backseat.

"If we could travel as the crow flies, it would probably turn out to be less than a mile. We have to start out from a location that isn't very close to our destination."

"And where do we have to start out?"

"Right in the middle of Hell's Kitchen."

"Where's that?"

Mallory smiled. "I guess it's no longer called Hell's Kitchen. Head down to 10th Avenue and go north."

After traveling a few blocks on 10th, she directed me to turn left on 49th.

"Midway down this block we'll cross a ravine that goes down thirty feet or so. When we get to that, park anywhere you can."

But there was no ravine.

"I guess it's been built over. Go down to 11th, take a left, then come back on 48th."

But there was no ravine on 48th either. We checked all the streets as far south as 42nd, then went back and started checking above 49th.

"A lot can happen to a city in two thousand years," I observed evenly.

"Yeah. I just hope we don't have to use a manhole."

I hoped so too but held my tongue.

We finally got a possible break on 51st, where a building had been demolished on the north side of the street.

"But this isn't midblock," I told her. In fact it was just a few doors west of 10th.

"The ravine wasn't midblock either. Trust me, this is right."

We parked, shrugged into our backpacks, and went over to the site of the demolished building, enclosed by an eight-foot chain-link fence.

"What now?" I asked.

"We go over the fence, of course."

"You're joking."

To demonstrate her seriousness, she scrambled over the fence, and said, "Come on, you can do it."

I did it, not easily or nimbly or gracefully, but there came a time when we were both once again on the same side of the fence. Now that I was there, I had a different impression of the situation. Just beyond the lip of the sidewalk was a drop of perhaps twelve or fifteen feet to a confused pile of rubble. Even Mallory wasn't foolhardy enough to leap into that. Following the side of the lot, we made our way to the back, which was still more or less at street level. Looking back from there, it was clear she was right. Fifty-first Street was a sort of shelf under which opened a dark trough-shaped portal extending almost the full width of the lot. We clambered down to it across twenty yards of debris of all kinds—masonry, timbers, pipes, wiring, lath, and plaster. Ducking under the lip of the street, we were then able to clamber down another fifteen yards to relatively solid ground, where two derelict railroad tracks disappeared into the tunnel ahead of us to the south.

"It's a tunnel now," Mallory noted and we walked on. "In my era—Gloria's era—it was a ravine open to the sky all the way to 42nd Street. And I think there was still train traffic on these rails. The whole city is like this."

"Like what?"

"It's all built over things that used to be in the open air. There are whole rivers down here they built over and forgot."

"You mean they're still running?"

"Sure, why not? They weren't dammed, they were just covered over and forgotten. All sorts of things were covered over and forgotten down here—ditches and canals dug and abandoned, subway lines built and scrapped. There's a whole world down here, probably bigger than the one above."

I looked up into the darker darkness overhead and tried to imagine being able to see the buildings of 48th Street, which is where we were by now, approximately.

Then, looking into the darkness ahead, I asked, "How do you know the way isn't blocked in front of us the way it's blocked behind us?"

"If it is, we'll just have to find another way down. There are a million ways. This is just the one I know best."

"We should have brought flashlights."

"That's what's in the backpacks, mostly. Two big ones and two hand-held types in each, plus replacement batteries."

"My God. Are you planning to set up camp?"

"No, I just wanted plenty of light."

We walked on. I asked, "Why don't we get a flashlight out now?"

"Because it's not dark yet. It's not anything *like* dark yet."

"I've got an apartment by the ruins of Carthage outside Tunis," I told her. "In the middle of the night, with all the drapes closed, it's not as dark as this."

"Your eyes'll get used to it. You'll see."

One set of tracks curved off to the left, and we followed them, leaving behind the natural stone walls of the ravine and entering an obviously *built* environment—built, but hardly orderly. Dredge up a ship from the bottom of the ocean, and this is what it would look like inside, except that traces of the shipbuilder's logic would inevitably remain. Here all was higgledy-piggledy and jury-rigged, put together with no guiding scheme, its original function unguessable.

Oddly enough, there was more light now. Our vista was wider. Passageways opened to the right and left, many of them lit by grates in the street twenty or thirty feet above. It was surprisingly quiet, the traffic overhead a distant thunder. The air was dank but not cold. The smell, being unlike anything I'd ever experienced, was indescribable. The delicately nurtured are protected from noxious odors, so we don't learn to name them. There were strains or veins of evil stink—rotting fruit, ancient mold, generations of rancid petroleum, I don't know—but this was no gut-wrenching sewer, at least as yet. To make up for the lack of sewer ambiance, however, there were plenty of rats, unruffled by our intrusion but giving way with thuggish sullenness.

I was following Mallory blindly and giving all my attention to avoiding the obstacles and entanglements that constituted the ground we were walking on. At some point, without my noticing it, we'd left the railroad tracks behind. After perhaps ten minutes of walking, we came to a distinctive, man-high object shaped like a fat torpedo. I call it distinctive because I'd never seen anything like it and couldn't begin to imagine its function. Beside it, inexplicably, was a twenty-foot length of battered chain-link fence, strung out toward no discernible destination, connecting to nothing, fencing nothing in or out. The whole place was like this, teeming with features that must have made sense to the people who put them there but that were now utterly meaningless.

The torpedo object and the fence were evidently land-marks for Mallory. We followed the fence till it staggered to an end, then turned right into an arched opening indistin-guishable from hundreds of others we'd passed. A round-sided tunnel stretched out ahead of us for perhaps thirty feet, where it opened into another room illuminated atmospheri-cally by a grate above. We never reached that room. Mallory paused at a metal portal set into the wall at the left. Although she scratched and tugged, it was rusted shut, and we had to go looking for tools to open it with. Tools were in endless supply down there, though few were as straightforward as crowbars or screwdrivers. There were hunks of metal that could be used to pry and bang, and we used them to pry and bang till the door fell off its hinges and we were able to crawl through into a vault impenetrably black except for a dim luminance leaking up from a grate in the floor. It appeared that this was our destination, or at least an intermediate one.

After pulling off the grate, she took a flashlight from my backpack, and showed me where we were heading. Five feet below the grate was a ledge some sixteen or eighteen inches wide. We were going to drop down to that ledge and follow it to that object over *there*, that object being a metal cabinet whose top was about eight feet below the ledge. We were going to drop down to the top of that cabinet and from there to the floor another six feet below.

I looked at the project without enthusiasm.

"What is this place, anyway?" I asked. "I mean, what's its significance to you?"

She shook her head impatiently, then abruptly dropped into the hole in front of us.

"Wait," I said. "Let me get a flashlight."

"You can take one from my pack once you get down here. Come on, I'll light the way."

She lit the way. When we got to the point where we had to drop down to the cabinet, she paused to play her flashlight over it.

"It looks all right," she said. "Another couple inches of dust, I guess."

But I was noticing something I hadn't seen before. There was a gap of about a foot between the cabinet and the wall. "We can't just hang over the edge and drop down to it," I pointed out.

"No, we have to jump."

"I'll go first," I said.

She smiled. "That's very gallant but not very practical. The rule is, lightest goes first." She stuck her flashlight inside her shirt and without ceremony jumped.

Terrifyingly, she crashed through the top of the cabinet but came to rest on some surface inside that was just a couple feet below.

"I'm all right," she said, pulling herself out of the hole she'd dug with her feet. "I'll go find some planks to cover the hole so you can jump."

She sat down on the edge of the cabinet then shoved off to reach the floor six feet below. First, she dragged over some crates to build a two-step stairway against the side of the cabinet, then she went hunting for planks. Luckily, things like crates and planks were as plentiful down there as clods of dirt in a cornfield, so it was only a matter of minutes before a substantial platform had been laid across the hole in the cabinet below me, and I was able to make the descent to the next level.

When Mallory insisted on dismantling the platform and stairway before moving on, I asked why.

"Just a habit," she said.

"Even habits have a point," I insisted.

"Call it superstition then, like throwing spilled salt over your shoulder."

I understood Mallory well enough by then to know I wasn't going to get any more out of her than that.

• • •

This level, which I had to suppose was at least three stories below street level, was naturally darker than the one above and even more cluttered with incomprehensible structures and rusting machinery. Dusty pipes ran in all directions like massed armies, enormous timbers lay in confused piles like pickup sticks, and rotting tubes and electrical conduit dangled from every surface like vines in a jungle. Mallory was leading us through a maze of tunnels, and it occurred to me that I was now hopelessly lost.

"Where are we?" I asked. "I mean in relation to what's aboveground."

"I'd say we're somewhere under the public library, assuming it's still where it was in 1952. Or we might be a little west of there."

After a few more zigs and zags, Mallory headed for what was to me just one more anomalous structure out of hundreds we'd passed, a flat-roofed shed surmounted by the remains of what had once been a pulley arrangement of some sort. The interior of the shed was closed off by a pair of matchboarded leaves sagging away from their strap hinges. When we tugged at them, they didn't so much come open as come off.

"Watch out," she warned, "there's no floor in there."

Indeed there was no floor but rather a six-foot-square shaft that appeared to go down about forty feet.

"I hope we're not going to jump this one," I said.

"No, there's a ladder attached to the wall over there at the right."

And so there was. Getting to it, however, would mean stepping across a chasm perhaps two feet wide. A distance of two feet doesn't sound like much, but the idea of crossing it over a forty-foot drop gave me a sickening twinge in my stomach.

"Aren't I clever?" Mallory said cheerily. "I brought some rope so we could lower our backpacks first."

We shrugged out of them, threaded the rope through the straps, and sent them to the bottom. Then, with my flash lighting the way, Mallory swung across the void and started down the ladder. The ladder, at least, looked solid enough, apparently made of some rustproof alloy.

While she was descending, I considered my situation. I didn't care for the idea of crossing the gap with a flashlight in one hand. I wanted both hands free for the business of grabbing the ladder, but I certainly wasn't going to make that grab in the dark. Since we had flashlights to spare, I decided to sacrifice one to illuminate the ladder while I was taking that big step. I dragged over a crate and positioned the flash to bounce light off the facing wall onto the ladder, so I wouldn't block it with my own body. Two minutes later, Mallory was down, and it was my turn. Ignoring the twinge, I stepped across and grabbed.

The ladder wobbled, or maybe I wobbled, I couldn't be absolutely sure which it was. The ladder was held away from the wall by a ten-inch brace. I stared at this brace, irresistibly contemplating the fact that the wooden plank it was screwed into was at least two thousand years old.

Well, it was bound to be fastened at lower points as well, where the wall would be stone. I looked back at the platform I'd just left. It was still there, just a step away. I'm afraid nothing but vanity decided the matter. I declined to lose face over a qualm that was probably groundless, so I began my descent.

Just below floor level, I saw there were indeed more braces, these screwed into masonry. The trouble was, I had enough light to see that, as I lowered my right foot to the next rung, the ladder shifted slightly to the left. As I lowered my left foot to the next rung, the ladder shifted slightly to the right. With every step, I was using the weight of my body to pull the ladder away from the wall. I decided to hurry. Keeping my body as close to the ladder as possible, I took three more steps down. One screw gave—I could feel it. A second followed quickly, then they all went in rapid succession like a burst of machine-gun fire as the ladder began to topple backward.

"I'm going to die now," I remember thinking.

But of course the ladder's yaw was broken by the other side of the shaft, leaving me dangling by my hands like an apple.

"Help," I croaked superfluously.

"You've got to get on the other side of the ladder," Mallory shouted up to me.

"I'd like to do that very much," I would have said if I'd had any breath. As it was, I just squawked, "How?"

"Wait, I'm coming."

I felt the ladder thrum as she climbed, on the "wrong" side, of course. I began to wonder how long I could actually hang on this way. Minutes seemed to pass, but it was probably just seconds.

Mallory reached between two rungs, grabbed my belt, and said, "Give me your right leg."

As I lifted it, she grabbed it and wrapped it around the side of the ladder. She switched hands at my belt, then asked for my left leg. When that was in place, she surveyed the situation and told me to put my left arm through the ladder and grab a rung as far down as I could reach. I did that.

"What we've got to do now is get you around the right side of the ladder. Can you scoot over to that side?" I could, but only by a few inches.

"Can you reach your right arm around to my side of the ladder?"

"Yes, but not very far."

"Get it around as far as the elbow."

I managed that, and she planted my right hand on a rung in front of her.

"Now we've just got to get the rest of you around here."

"My left leg is the problem."

"Yeah, I can see that. Here's what we'll do. I'll unwrap it and help you put it on a rung on your side of the ladder. Can you do that?"

"I guess so."

When we got that done, she said, "Can you move some more to your right? We've got to get your arm around as far as the armpit."

"Help me move my left leg some more." I managed to use my left arm, looped over a rung in front of me, to take a little weight off it.

I was now basically hanging off the side of the ladder.

"Now we just have to put your right hand where my right hand is, then you'll be able to pull yourself around."

"Where will *you* be?"

"As soon as we get your right hand connected to the side rail, I'll get out of the way."

On her way down, she paused to twist my right foot around so it was toed in on the rung. It was an awkward situation but not nearly as awkward as falling thirty feet in the dark, so I managed to heave myself around. The trouble was, as soon as I did, my legs turned to rubber, and I had to hang there like a scarecrow for ten minutes till they started feeling like legs again and I could begin a wobbly descent.

Mallory used the interval to organize a reception, creating a small dining alcove lit by the larger flashlights, which were designed for area illumination. She sat me down on a crate and handed me a chocolate bar, which I ingested in not much more than a single gulp.

"I'm sorry," she said matter-of-factly.

"You didn't know it was going to happen."

"No, I didn't."

"I hope there are no more thrills like that one in store for us."

"No, nothing like that," she said ambiguously.

I looked up at the scene of my narrow escape and asked how we were going to get back.

"Oh, we're not going back *that* way."

"Obviously."

"I mean that was never the intention."

"You mean we could have come a different way?"

"Of course. There are hundreds. This is just the one I know."

"If this is the one you know, then how do we get out?"

"Getting out is entirely different."

"How so?"

She thought about that and said, "It's like a parking garage. The trick is finding your car, not getting out. You can't miss getting out—once you've found the car."

"I see what you're saying."

"Right now, you could find your way back without me—just take any opening that heads upward. But without me, you'd never find the place where we're going."

"I get it."

"Are you ready to go on? It's not far now."

I said that was good news and dragged myself up.

2 3

WE WERE NOW beyond all reach of light from the surface, and as we continued to thread our way through the maze, the beams of our flashlights turned the region into a dancing maelstrom of shadows.

"This is probably an extremely silly question," I said, "but are we headed for one specific spot you know about?"

"Of course," she replied. "Why would you think otherwise?"

"Because you can't possibly know exactly where you are."

"What makes you think that?"

"It's beyond belief that this chaos could be recognizable to you after two thousand years."

"From my point of view, it's more like two weeks."

"But it can't possibly be the same now as it was then."

Mallory paused in front of a rectangular niche, big enough to hold a couple of refrigerators. I call it a niche, but this implies a function the space may never have had.

"Do you know what was going on here two thousand years ago?"

"You mean right here in this niche? I have no idea, obviously."

"It was a little flower stall, run by a girl named Shirley."

"I don't believe it."

"You don't? When Shirley went broke, it was taken over by a guy who had a line of handmade chocolates. Then later there was a guy dealing three-card monte, and after that a couple of rack-fillers used it as a warehouse."

"Okay, I understand that none of this is true. What's your point?"

"The point is that two thousand years ago, this niche was as empty as it is today, and for the same reason. It's absolutely useless for any imaginable purpose. No one uses it, no one wants it, no one changes it. The same is true of everything down here." She flashed her light on a coil of conduit that lay at our feet, one bit of trash in the midst of thousands. "Why don't you move that?" she asked.

"Why should I?"

"Exactly—why should you? Why should anyone? No one's moved it in two thousand years, and no one's *going* to move it. Come back in a thousand years and it'll still be right here."

"I see what you mean," I said.

A few minutes later we were heading down a long, round-sided tunnel like dozens we'd traversed and hundreds we'd passed. As in many, a bundle of pipes of various sizes ran down its length, held in place at shoulder height by heavy metal straps. Mallory was interested in this particular bundle, however, and was following it with her flashlight.

About midway down the course of this tunnel, the biggest of the pipes—perhaps thirty inches in diameter—was joined by another the same size coming through the wall beside it. As was usually the case down there, the work done to put this pipe through the curved wall of the tunnel wasn't elegantly executed. A generous-sized hole had been punched through the masonry, and that was that. No one had troubled to fill the gap above the pipe. Why would they? There was room enough to shove a small suitcase through on its side—except that, as Mallory explained it, we weren't going to be shoving any suitcases through the gap, we were going to be shoving ourselves through it.

Forestalling the objection I was about to make, she said, "This is the destination, Jason. We're there. It's ten feet away."

I could hardly dig in my heels over ten feet, so I said, "Okay."

She hesitated for a moment, then added, "This is no joke."

"I didn't say it was a joke. I said okay."

There was just enough light to see her shake her head. "You're going to think I'm playing with you, but I'm not."

"What the hell are you talking about?"

Instead of answering, she hoisted herself up onto the pipe and worked her way into the hole, pushing her backpack in front of her. It was time to get seriously dirty.

I waited till I was sure I wasn't going to get kicked in the face, then I slipped out of my own backpack, stowed my flashlight, and followed her example, heading in a direction I identified as vaguely east. There was one spot where my head would go through, provided my cheek was sliding in the dust on top of the pipe. With my arms inside, I had to apply first elbows then hands to the interior wall to propel the rest of me in up to my hips, at which point I seemed to be stuck. My legs, still outside, had nothing to push against, and my hands had nothing to grab onto except the dusty pipe I was lying on. I eventually adopted a sort of caterpillar wriggle, lifting my chest, bringing my stomach forward, and using that to propel me an inch or two at a time. I soon worked a knee through the opening, and it was easy after that. I wondered how Mallory had managed it so effortlessly, sliding through the hole like an eel.

Now that I was finished huffing and puffing my way through the wall, I noticed that the silence around me was absolute. Mallory and her flashlight beacon were nowhere in sight. I switched on my own flashlight and looked around. The pipe I'd crawled in on continued in its eastward course, disappearing into a wall three feet ahead, and nothing bigger than a rat could have followed it. Behind me, the wall of the tunnel curved up and away into a ceiling four feet away. The floor below, obviously the same as the floor of the tunnel we'd just left, made a north-south passageway running parallel to the tunnel.

As far as I could see, Mallory had vanished into thin air.

At last I understood why I might think she was playing with me. In fact, I was about one-third convinced she *was* playing with me. More to the point, however, I was two-thirds afraid that maybe she *wasn't* playing with me—that she'd fallen into some hidden chasm and was gone forever.

I called out her name but got nothing back except echoes.

She'd said ten feet. Having crossed two of them to get to the middle of this passageway, there were presumably eight still to go. I slid down off the pipe and began digging through the junk on the floor, looking for trapdoors. There were none, of course. I checked the pipe itself for openings on the underside. There were none. Mallory had snuck in a reference to Eddie Tucker's "loose brick," so I looked for loose bricks in the east wall of the passageway. There were none. I played my flashlight over the ceiling without getting any more bright ideas than I'd had the first time. Resting atop the masonry of the tunnel like a board on a cylinder, the ceiling presented a smooth, unbroken surface.

I was reluctant to call out again—reluctant to admit I was stuck—but if she was honest in her ten-foot estimate, then that's what I was. I thought of a way to end the standoff without humiliating myself. Speaking in a perfectly normal tone of voice, I said, "I'm beginning to think you're playing with me."

"Turn off the flashlight," Mallory replied. Her voice bounced off the walls in a way that left me clueless as to its point of origin, but I couldn't resist sending my light around again anyway, hoping to catch her hovering in midair, perhaps. No wiser, I turned it off.

For a moment I was blind. Then, as the rods and cones of my eyes gradually came to an agreement about the situation, I perceived an arm reaching into the darkness from a spot where no arm could be. It was apparently issuing from the juncture between the ceiling and the tunnel some four feet above and four feet to the north of the pipe we'd come in on.

"Do you see it?" Mallory asked.

"I see it."

She withdrew her arm. Switching on my flashlight and directing it to the spot, all I now perceived was that no one could possibly be there. I climbed up on the pipe, then flattened myself onto the upper curve of the tunnel wall. From this position I could now see the opening Mallory's voice was coming from.

"Get as much of your body as you can above the middle of the bulge," she advised.

That made wonderful sense from a theoretical point of view, but turning theory into practice was a different matter. Standing on tiptoe, I was able to embrace a lot of the tunnel wall, and that was fine, but I couldn't lift my feet off the pipe without sliding back down.

"Wait a second," Mallory said. "I'm trying to think how I do it myself. Start with your left leg."

"Start how?"

"It's sort of like getting up on a horse. You need to throw your left leg up over the bulge. Then climb up and to your right, pulling your right leg up. You need to end up lying stretched out above the bulge. After that, it's easy."

She was right, provided you were talking about a horse the size of an elephant and were meant to ride not sitting on top but lying on one side of it. I managed to get up there and once in position felt secure enough to creep forward toward Mallory's hand, visible four feet away.

Mallory was reaching down through an opening just above the juncture of the ceiling and the apex of the tunnel. To someone on the floor below, the bulge of the tunnel wall not only hid this opening, it persuaded the eye that no such opening could exist. There just wasn't room for such an opening, so it was pointless to look for one.

Struggling through this opening, about twelve inches wide by twenty-four long, I found myself in a low-ceilinged, windowless, doorless room some eighteen feet square. Again, to call it a room is misleading. It was a leftover space, a purposeless and unintended volume created by the random intersection of six unrelated surfaces, and the fact that it could serve as a room was the sheerest accident.

Mallory added the area light from my backpack to the one she'd already set up. Without these lights, the room would have been as dark as the Carlsbad Caverns' deepest pit. With them, it was surprisingly homelike. There were two or three makeshift chairs, a few crate tables showing signs of what might have been recent use if they hadn't been covered in a thick layer of dust. There was a sizable sleeping pallet, which had been laid out on a pair of pallets of the kind used for storing cargo. Only later did I realize that all this furniture had been disassembled below and reassembled here once the parts had been passed through the narrow entrance to the room.

"What is this place?" I asked.

"This is where I spent the last three months of my life as Gloria MacArthur."

Mallory returned my gawk with a cool, passionless gaze. Then she turned away to an area where she'd arranged two chairs and a crate table.

"Sit down," she said. I saw that she'd cleared the chairs of the bulk of the dust they'd collected over the centuries, not that it mattered much, considering the filth we'd picked up in the last hour.

She sat down and started disassembling the crate with a rusty screwdriver she'd found somewhere. When she had the top off, she tipped it at an angle like a conjuror so I could see it was empty. Then she went back to work, taking it apart piece by piece till she was ready to make her next revelation. The crate had a false bottom, a space twenty-four inches square by four inches deep, packed solid with small bundles fitted together with painstaking precision to maximize the available room.

"Our treasury," she said. "The collected remains of two lives." She reached for one of the larger bundles, wrapped in what looked like oilcloth, explaining that they'd had room for only one book. She unwrapped it just enough to be able to flip through the pages till she came to a snapshot, which she handed me.

It showed a grinning African girl, a skinny sixteen-year-old, cute as a proverbial button, all nappy hair, blazing white teeth, and eyes as big as saucers.

"Who is this?" I asked.

"That's Gloria MacArthur."

I reeled.

2 4

I WAS AS MUCH staggered by my own blindness as anything else. What else had she been preparing me for but this?

Staggered or not, before I could stop myself, I glanced up from the face in the photo to Mallory's face, checking the resemblance as an entirely automatic reflex. She caught the glance, understood its point, and laughed, uncannily creating a resemblance I wouldn't have seen there two hours before, when her face was still clean and lily white. Now it was closer to being black than the grinning face in the snapshot.

She took back the photo, replaced it between the pages, and started to shove the book into her backpack when I asked her what book it was. She turned back the oilcloth to expose the cover. It was something called *The New Negro*.

"It was a very influential book in the twenties and thirties, even in the forties," she explained. "Influential but also controversial. The guy who put it together had a tendency to see the 'New Negro' as someone who was *almost* white, as someone who had cut off his cultural roots well above such low life things as jazz and blues. The New Negro was expected to be much more drawn to Beethoven and Bach than to Billie Holiday and Bessie Smith. All the same, it had some valuable stuff in it that no one wanted to lose."

"Who is this 'we' you keep referring to?"

Mallory rewrapped the book and put it in her backpack before giving me an answer. "I'm not going to let you piece the story together through interrogation," she said. "I'll tell it my own way."

"Of course. That's fine."

The woman had a positive knack for putting me in the wrong before I even had a chance to *go* wrong.

"I'm not going to spend a lot of time telling you things you already know," she began. "Americans weren't crushed by losing the war, because they didn't think of it as losing. Hitler's scientists had beaten ours to the atomic bomb by a matter of months, and that was all it took. The planned Allied invasion was called off in a hurry, and a cease-fire was in place practically overnight. Germany had the whip in its hand but was too exhausted to use it. The United States was out of the war without ever having been bombed, invaded, or even threatened.

"It was different for the people of Europe, of course. Places like France, Belgium, and the Netherlands became virtual provinces of Germany. Great Britain barely talked its way out of being occupied. Those were the losers. The Americans weren't losers, they just hadn't quite managed to be winners. It was time to pick up the pieces and move on. People were glad to forget about it.

"Nobody officially 'knew' what had happened to the Jews. There were rumors about death camps, places like Buchenwald and Belsen and Dachau, but it gradually came to be believed that these rumors were being manufactured by the Jews themselves. The Jews were doing their best to keep alive hatred of the Hun—this is the way it was perceived, the way we were *encouraged* to perceive it. The Jews weren't going to let things get back to 'normal.' They wanted the war to go on. I'm sure your little girls would have no difficulty explaining that."

"That's right. They wouldn't."

"I'm talking about the middle to late forties here, the years when television was just beginning to catch on. Writers for this new medium were producing a lot of cheap spy melodrama, and it was handy to have a ready-made class of enemies to draw on. Gradually this class of enemies became more and more distinctly Jews. It wasn't necessary to *call* them Jews. You could identify them by their names, their clothes, their profiles, their accents. These were the people the good guys were always struggling with, always on the verge of losing to.

"I'm sure you know that life imitates art. The gangsters of the thirties and early forties learned all their moves from the movies. In the late forties, all the gangsters in the movies were Jews. No one was surprised if in real life the papers reported that police had 'broken up a gang,' and it turned out to be a 'Jewish' gang. Arresting Jews came to be seen as working against crime. The Jews were hiding out. Of course they were hiding out—they were criminals! By 1948 you didn't have to have a specific crime to charge a Jew with. If he was hiding out—and they were all hiding out—then he was a criminal, and tracking him down and locking him up automatically made the world a better place.

"The Jews *we* knew were different, of course. These were artists, not criminals. Then one day Mark Rothko and Adolph Gottlieb disappeared—both on the same day. Two or three of the guys said, 'Well, this is some kind of mistake,' and they went downtown to talk to the police about it. They ended up in the office of some captain, who looked at them with great interest and said, 'Oh, so you know these two men, do you? Close associates, are you?' He made his point very clear, and by the time the guys left, they were practically saying they'd never heard of Rothko and Gottlieb. Eventually all the Jews were taken—guys like Barnett Newman, Herbert Ferber, and Seymour Lipton. Lee Krasner wasn't taken, she killed herself.

"By the late forties, as I said, the gangsters were all Jews, according to the movies—but their thugs were all blacks. They made very willing thugs, you see, being glad to have a chance to get back at their former slave-masters. The new language of film made it clear that blacks were all seething with rage and ready to rise up to murder white folks whenever their Jewish handlers gave the word.

"More and more white politicians and pundits were telling us that if us colored folks didn't like it here, maybe we should get ourselves back to Africa, and more and more of us were thinking that maybe this wasn't such a bad idea.

Wholesale deportations began in 1950. The word was given out that the people of Africa were longing to have us back and were preparing a regular paradise for us. Of course, not all Negroes were going to be deported—that's the word that was being given out. The *worthy* ones, the ones who were really *contributing* something, were welcome to stay. Naturally Roy and I saw ourselves as falling into that category— we were artists, after all, not thugs.

"But by the end of 1951 people like us were getting nervous. No one was hearing from friends and relatives who had returned to the Old Country, and it was beginning to be rumored that ships carrying deportees were never arriving. Government officials pooh-poohed all this, of course, producing carloads of happy letters supposedly received in this country from emigrants.

"Among the 'worthy' Negroes who were not being deported were officials of the NAACP—the National Association for the Advancement of Colored People. One of these officials, executive secretary Walter White, announced that he was going to pay a visit to Africa to see for himself what was going on. The government said it couldn't give him a visa, because, as the law was written by then, if you left, you couldn't come back, no matter what—if you were a Negro. White said, 'All right, we'll send Delia Tremayne. I'll take her word for it.' Delia Tremayne was a prominent white socialite who'd been a supporter of the NAACP since the thirties.

"The government now came back and said, 'Look, this is all completely unnecessary. We've been making a film record of resettlement in Africa ever since it started. Once you see this film, all your doubts will vanish. Just give us a little more time. We weren't planning to release it for a year or more, but we'll start editing it together right away. Till then, for God's sake, don't rock the boat, because that would only make it worse for your people.' We were always being told about what we shouldn't do because it would 'make things worse for our people.' We shouldn't hold protest meetings or take out ads in the papers or organize marches. We should be really, really polite and take it on the chin and smile a big smile and never complain, then we might go on being counted among the Negroes who were 'worthy' of being treated like scum in the land of the free and the home of the brave.

"The government now began offering special inducements to Negroes willing to emigrate immediately. They began filling ships with blacks faster than they'd filled them with troops during the war. Walter White continued to press for the promised film. The government continued to procrastinate. Finally White gave them an ultimatum. He was booking a March 1, 1953, flight to Africa for Delia Tremayne and two of her friends, and if the government wanted to stop them, they'd have to release this film. On February 28, White was arrested, charged with fomenting an uprising, the NAACP was formally disbanded, and Delia Tremayne and her friends were told not to bother showing up at the airport.

"Nothing had changed, the government said. There was no crisis. Everything was okay. What was vitally important was to get us back where we belonged as soon as possible, before the American people lost patience with us in a big way. The fact is, there were still too many of us to risk a direct and open confrontation.

"Roy and I were sure by now that no blacks were actually

being resettled in Africa. We didn't know what was happening to them, but they certainly weren't ending up in the arms of distant aunts and uncles in their ancient homeland. We began to make our plans.

"Roy was a photographer, and an unusual one. People said he could see in the dark, and what you saw in his pictures was, in a sense, what he saw in the dark. There's a bundle of his negatives here, though I don't know whether they survived or not. We did what we could to protect them, but . . ." Mallory shrugged. "We weren't thinking of two thousand years. We weren't thinking of two hundred years. We were just doing the best we could. Anyway . . . Roy knew about New York underground. He was fascinated by New York underground, and he knew there was nothing in the world like it as a hiding place. He said we could disappear down here and never be found in a thousand years. He actually said that: a thousand years.

"We moved into the tunnels in April, but we weren't anywhere near this deep at that point. The trouble was, we weren't the only people with this idea. More and more blacks were slipping into the tunnels, but they weren't prepared the way we were. They were in and out, in and out, and it didn't take the police that long to figure out what was going on. In a way, it even made their work easier, because they could gun people down in the tunnels with no witnesses, no fuss. No one doubted this was justified. Those people wouldn't be down there if they weren't criminals.

"Roy and I kept going deeper and deeper . . ."

"Tell me," I said. "What were you hoping for?"

"That's a good question. We could never quite believe there was no hope. We kept thinking, 'Somebody's gonna put a stop to this. Somebody's gonna say, "Wait a second, what's going on here?"' We had *friends* up there, y'know? Or people we thought of as friends. We kept thinking, 'They're not gonna let this happen to us. Not to *us!*' That's why we had to hang on. One of those days we were gonna hear the 'All Clear' signal, and it'd be over. It had to happen. We just had to hang on. And this room is where we ended up hanging on."

"But what did you live on?"

"That was the catch, of course. We couldn't just *stay* here. We had to go back up to the surface every two or three days. I suppose we could've tried living on the rats. I don't know. I think we felt that if it came to a choice between living on the rats or not living at all, we'd just rather not live at all.

"When you and I leave, we'll take the route that leads to Grand Central Station. We're literally just a few minutes away from the hotel. But Roy and I couldn't use that route. The police had that covered. That's why I never learned the route *in* from Grand Central Station. We always went in and out by the route you and I followed today. I know you didn't believe me, but I could have followed it blindfolded. I knew every inch of it."

"What was the situation on the surface by this time?"

"By this time, it was all out in the open. If you were spotted by the police, you were whisked off to a concentration camp on Staten Island and you never came back."

"So you couldn't show your faces when you came up?"

"Christ, no."

"But what did you do then? How did you find food?"

Mallory shrugged. "Tons of perfectly good food get thrown out every night in New York City, and at three o'clock in the morning, nobody's paying much attention to where it goes. And there were still a few people who considered us friends. The trouble was, we became famous—or legendary. You know what New York City's like. There came a time when there wasn't a single black man, woman, or child left in the city—but what about those two living seven levels down under the tracks of Grand Central Station? This is what our friends told us. Half the city believed we were just a legend, like the alligators, but the other half believed we were real. The police liked the idea of finding us—or even just searching for us. It was great publicity. Someone got the bright idea of using dogs to track us. This was bad news, because we'd been leaving a trail for months, laying down a scent back and forth two or three times a week. We began spending our days laying false trails and circular trails, figuring they'd lose faith in the dogs eventually. Then the newspapers began promoting a rivalry between two professionals who were involved. Each saw a chance of getting some national headlines if he tracked us down.

"At this point we lost touch with what was happening aboveground. We knew we couldn't risk going back. That was finished, so we got down to making some plans for how it was going to end. We knew we could buy a few more days or weeks of life by allowing ourselves to be taken, but neither one of us wanted that. Water wasn't a problem. There are plenty of ways to get water down here. The problem was food. It was a strange situation. We didn't want them to find us ever, but if they didn't find us soon, we'd starve to death. We weren't going to let them take us alive, but we didn't want to starve to death. In the end we had to swallow our finer feelings and go for the rats. Of course, you can't live forever on rat meat and water, we knew that. We thought maybe the trackers would give up. We didn't think at all. We just got through one day at a time.

"We knew where the trackers were pretty much all the time, especially if they were getting close. Once they found the right tunnel, they'd spot the pipe right away. We tried filling in the gap but the only way to do that was to lay bricks on top of the pipe, and this would be spotted right away. We had to leave it the way it was and hope they'd miss it. After all, there are a million cracks and holes down here. But of course the pipe we'd crawled across going in and out hundreds of times would be like a beacon to dogs.

"Once they found the pipe they'd find the passageway inside. We had to give them somewhere to go once they were in the passageway. There's a way out of the passageway to the north, and we laid down a heavy track to that exit and beyond, but there's only so far you can take that sort of thing. Eventually you have to go back, and that's where the track ends and the tracker realizes he's been had.

"Rigging an alarm system was a little tricky, since it couldn't just make a noise, it had to do something I could see or feel, but we managed it. We didn't have anything else to do, after all. It had two stages. We'd know if someone came in on the pipe, and we'd know if he started climbing across the tunnel wall to the entrance to this room. We knew the first alarm would probably be tripped someday, but we hoped the second one would never be. We had a door we could close once we got inside here—a sort of a plug that looked like masonry from down below. It was impossible to spot visually, but if anyone ever got the idea of letting a dog check the area above the bulge of the tunnel, then we were finished.

"The day came when the first alarm was triggered. We had a gun, and after that it was always in easy reach. A week went by, then the second alarm went off and we used the gun."

Seeing the question in my eyes, she shook her head. "I'm not going to talk about that."

Almost involuntarily, I looked over my shoulder.

"They took the bodies away, obviously," Mallory went on. "I suppose they could hardly leave them here. How would they be able to claim their great victory without the trophies?"

"I'm sorry," I said, inadequately.

"I'm through calling you a murderer, Jason. It doesn't do me any good, and it certainly doesn't do you any good. You might as well apologize for killing Julius Caesar."

We wouldn't need the area lights again, so we left them behind to make room in our backpacks for the various bundles from "the treasury." These included items like letters, address books, checkbooks, passports, diaries, photo albums, a bundle of news clippings that fell to dust at a touch, a few pieces of heirloom jewelry that might have brought two or three hundred dollars at a pawnshop, and a stack of photo-negatives in glassine sleeves. Flattened out at the very bottom were six drawings and nine lithographs from artists whose names I would later learn: Charles White, Augusta Savage, Arshile Gorky, and Adolph Gottlieb, among others

In an obscurely symbolic gesture, we left the area lights burning when we left.

As Mallory had said, we were surprisingly close to Grand Central Station. It may, in fact, have been virtually straight up, though it wasn't possible for us to take a route straight up. Well within half an hour, we were sauntering alongside platforms still populated with late-afternoon commuters, who stared at us as if we were visiting Martians. When we made our way into the lobby of the hotel, the reaction was even more dramatic, and it wasn't easy to persuade the management that two people who would've been ejected from a coal-miners' saloon could be a distinguished citizen and a paying guest. They wouldn't have been happy admitting even an emperor who seemed to exude black filth the way a soaked sponge exudes water. I'm sure we dirtied the walls just by walking past them.

Once we reached Mallory's suite, I was able to indulge in one of the simple pleasures of the rich. I called home and arranged for a servant to deliver a complete change of clothes and a suitcase with other necessaries.

From certain indications, spoken and unspoken, I'd gathered I was expected to spend the night.

PART THREE

RISEN

The dead, as we have
seen, can quite literally
emerge from their graves
if the conditions are right.

2 **5**

LIKE DINNER the night before, we had breakfast served in the room. Over coffee, I asked Mallory what she thought we should do.

"About what?"

"Maybe that's my real question. What is there we can do anything about?"

She raised her eyebrows at me innocently. "I have no idea what you're getting at."

I spent some time thinking about how to explain it, then finally said, "At the Gramercy Academy, you learned some things you couldn't live without. You needed to know those things so you could get on with your life."

"Very true," she agreed.

"Yesterday I learned some things I couldn't live without, though I didn't previously know they were there to be learned. Now I'm wondering how I'm going to get on with *my* life."

"I see. I *guess* I see."

"So I ask you what you think we should do."

"I don't think *I* need to do anything, Jason. If *you* need to do something, you're the only one who knows what it is."

"That's so," I said. "I've thought of a couple things, and I wondered if you'd thought of any."

"I'm not looking, Jason. To be honest, all I was thinking about was finding studio space in Manhattan."

"We can do that," I conceded. "But there are some things I have to do as well."

She shrugged, as if to say, *well, go do them*.

I put in a call to the newspaper that advertises itself as the world's oldest continuously published daily, where an acquaintance from school days, Ward Woolton, had attained some sort of editorial position on the city desk. When I got through the telephone net, I was informed (in a tone that suggested I should know better) that Mr. Woolton would not be available until ten-thirty at the earliest. Then I called Mother to see if she could give me the name of Dad's bookseller.

"Which one? He has several."

"I'm thinking of the one who provided him with the first-edition M.R. James that pleased him so much." Among his other eccentricities, Father is a passionate collector of Victorian ghost stories.

"That was Edmund Dial. He has a shop on Lexington in the Fifties."

With my mother, to inquire is to be informed.

I made a phone call and learned that the shop was open, though Mr. Dial wasn't in as yet, his schedule being similar to Ward Woolton's. No matter. I took a cab to Hell's Kitchen, retrieved my car, and headed for Lexington and 54th. Dial's establishment was far too grand to be called a shop, having six high-ceilinged stories packed solid with literary collectibles.

I didn't have to do more than mention my name to have the clerk's undivided attention. I asked if perhaps I could await Mr. Dial's arrival in his office, if he had such a thing. Certainly he did have such a thing, and certainly I was welcome to have a seat in it. And use the telephone to make a local call? Positively.

Ward Woolton had reached his desk at the world's oldest daily, though he didn't sound overjoyed to hear from me. We hadn't been bosom pals, just classmates. After exchanging the usual formalities and pleasantries, I asked if he was in a position to discuss a news story.

"That is, in fact, exactly the position I'm in here at the *Times*," he informed me dryly." I'm here for no other purpose."

"Could I drop by and see you this afternoon then?" I asked.

"Not this afternoon, unless you're calling from a burning building or a crime scene."

"Nothing like that," I admitted. "Tomorrow morning?"

"Can you give me a hint? About the story, I mean. Is it something to do with the Tull family?"

"No, it has nothing to do with the family."

"I trust you're not just going to tell me you've found the girl of your dreams and are going to get married."

"No, of course not."

"Then how about it?"

"Let me ask a question back," I told him. "Has it ever occurred to you to wonder if the history we teach our children is a lie?"

After a moment of stunned silence, he said, "Good Lord, Jason. I hope you're joking."

"Why?"

"Surely that's manifest."

"It isn't to me."

"You've *been* there, Jason. We were there together. It's *all* lies and bullshit till graduate school. Why else *have* graduate school?"

"That's very cynical."

"Is it?"

"Suppose I were to tell you that the lies don't stop in graduate school."

"Golly, Jason, what great truth are you going to reveal to me? That the earth is hollow and inhabited by the survivors of Atlantis? That the human race is an experiment in sociology being run by little green men on Mars?"

"I haven't lost my mind, Ward. Give me an hour and I'll convince you of that."

"An hour? Christ, what do you think this is, the reading room of the British Museum? This is a newspaper. If you can't convince me in five minutes that you've got something I can use, then you don't *have* something I can use. It's as simple as that."

"All right, give me five minutes."

"I'll gladly give you five minutes, Jason, but, please, no

bullshit about the lies of history. That's not news, that's just blather."

I said I understood, and we made a date for eleven the following morning.

Edmund Dial, when he made his appearance a few minutes later, was nothing like I'd vaguely expected, an elderly gentleman with a bookish stoop and dusty clothes, but rather a trim, sharp-faced man in his mid-forties, dressed rather more smartly than I was. Though he came through the door wearing a smile intended for my father, he quickly recovered when he realized his mistake, not discarding the smile but ratcheting it down to a more appropriate level.

He asked if I would join him in a cup of coffee, and I naturally said I'd be delighted. Having used the family name as a calling card, I had to endure the attendant ceremonials. He summoned an assistant, issued instructions, and looked as if he had to restrain himself from sending her off with a clap of the hands. When the rituals had been attended to, and sufficient time had passed, he asked what he could do for me.

I said, "I suppose you've seen and handled every kind of book there is."

He raised an eyebrow but agreed that this was so. "There are collectors," he added gravely, "for *every* type of book."

I took out Mallory's copy of *The New Negro*, which I'd been carrying in an envelope, and handed it to him. He recoiled, not so much from its title, I felt, as from its condition, which was that of any old, heavily used book. Lifting the cover with his fingertips, he scanned the copyright page, shook his head faintly, and asked why I was showing it to him.

"You said there are collectors for every type of book. I was wondering if there are any collectors for *this* type."

He gave me a frosty smile. "You caught me in an over-statement, Mr. Tull. I assumed you were hinting at some variety of erotica. There are hundreds of thousands of old books that no one wants—no one at all—and this is one of them."

"So you wouldn't sell a book a like this."

"I'd be glad to sell it if there were someone to buy it. As it is, if it belonged to me, I'd throw it in the trash. I trash thousands of books a year, Mr. Tull, books received when entire collections and libraries are sold in a single lot."

He handed me back the book.

"I take it that merely being two thousand years old doesn't make it valuable."

"Certainly not. Any pebble on the street is thousands of years old. That doesn't make it valuable."

"But surely there are *some* two-thousand-year-old books that are valuable."

"Of course," he said, beginning to look bored. "You've seen many such books in your father's collection."

"What distinguishes one from the other?"

He gave me a look of frank disgust. "The valuable books are the ones people want, of course. The worthless ones are the ones no one wants."

"But how can you tell just by looking that no one wants this book?"

"That's how I make my living, Mr. Tull. It's my *business* to recognize books that are wanted, and *The New Negro* isn't one of them, I assure you."

"I'm afraid you're going to have to revise your estimate, Mr. Dial. *The New Negro* has joined the ranks of the wanted. *I* want it."

"Well," he said, with a bit of a smirk, "luckily, you have it."

"And I want others."

He frowned. "Others of what kind? Books about Negroes?"

"Not necessarily."

"Then what? You can't simply want all the books I discard. They don't constitute a *type*. All they have in common is that no one wants them."

"Let me think for a minute," I told him. "I assume you know who Adolf Hitler was."

"Of course. The so-called Hero of Dachau. A semi-legendary character, I assume, like William Tell."

"Actually, he was a historical person."

Mr. Dial shrugged.

"I wouldn't be surprised if someone wrote a biography of him in English during the Great War."

"Why do you stress 'in English'?"

"The English-speaking nations were Hitler's enemies during the Great War."

Mr. Dial looked as if he were being led into deep water. "So," he said meditatively, "you're looking for a biography of the Hero of Dachau as written from an enemy point of view—a Jewish point of view, in other words."

"Why do you say that? I mean, why Jewish in particular?"

"Because most of the publishing houses of England and America at the time were in Jewish hands. I assume that's how *this* book came to be published," he said, nodding at *The New Negro*. "Obviously no one but a Jew would care to publish such a thing."

"Perhaps that's the guideline we're looking for, then—books published by Jews."

Finally Mr. Dial knew he was dealing with a madman. He stared at me blankly, hopelessly, perhaps wondering if he would ever be called upon to repeat this lunatic conversation to my father.

"For the moment," I pressed on, "do me this favor. Let me root around in your discards. It can't do any harm, and if I find something I want, you can set any price on it you think is fair."

For half a second he thought he would balk at this suggestion; then it seemed to occur to him that it was a way to get me out of his office. A few minutes later, I was in a vast underground chamber where two young women were engaged in the apparently endless task of separating newly acquired lots of books into valuable and worthless. It looked like nasty, boring work, but my presence and my quixotic enterprise provided some welcome amusement for them.

After three hours, I realized I was working too much in the dark. I'd made two finds that seemed remarkably lucky: an antiwar novel called *All Quiet on the Western Front*, translated from the German, and one called *It Can't Happen Here*, about the possibility of a fascist takeover in the United States. I also selected an incomprehensible little item called *Three Lives*, by someone named Gertrude Stein, just because I felt sure Mr. Dial would say no one but a Jew would care to publish such a thing. I unearthed but ultimately left behind a few books by authors with notionally Jewish names like

Steinbeck and Dreiser, figuring they could wait till I knew more.

When I submitted my treasures to Mr. Dial for valuation, he was torn, feeling that in good conscience he could neither make me a gift of such rubbish nor charge me for it. We deferred the problem till later by opening an account for me, listing the three items as having a value "to be determined."

Returning to the hotel, I learned that Mallory was off touring spaces on offer as artists' studios. I settled down with the phone to find someone who might know how to deal with two-thousand-year-old photo negatives. Most experts assured me they would be beyond salvation, but I finally tracked down a technological archeologist who said she knew a trick or two that others might not and agreed to have a look at them.

After Mallory returned and had a bath, we tackled the grave matter of where to dine. I made a number of suggestions, but she finally decided she didn't want to "make a production out of it," so we ended up in a dining room downstairs.

In the middle of our second cocktail, I told her I couldn't imagine not asking her to marry me.

"That's a strange way to put it," she replied. "Are you asking or just making conversation?"

"I'm asking."

She took out time to have a sip of her drink. "Actually, I know what you mean. I also couldn't imagine your not asking me."

"Are you accepting or just making conversation?"

"So far," she said, "I'm just making conversation."

"I see," I said, in my owlish way.

"You know that scrawny black chick you saw in the photo yesterday? That's me."

"I realize that."

"I slept with half the guys in the Club before I hooked up with Roy. Can you stand that?"

"That was two thousand years ago, Mallory."

"To me, it was last year. I'm that person."

"Okay, but I'm also some other 'that person,' you know. We just don't happen to know what person it was. Maybe I was one of the guys who tracked you down to that tunnel."

She wasn't buying this. "If you were one of those guys, you aren't him now. But I *am* that girl in the photo, I guarantee it."

"I love you whatever girl you are, Mallory. It's you I love, not a photograph."

"Love is too much for me right now, Jason. That's just the way it is."

"I understand. I'm not trying to push you."

"I know you aren't. We're having fun, and that's a good start. Even yesterday was fun, in its own weird way."

"I liked the part where I was hanging off that ladder thirty feet in the air."

"I did too."

We were back in the suite by nine-thirty and having a nightcap when the phone rang. Mallory answered it and reported that a visitor downstairs was asking to come up, one Harry Whitaker.

"Harry Whitaker!"

"Who's Harry Whitaker?"

"An old friend of the family. Do you want to have him up? It's entirely up to you."

Mallory told the desk clerk to send him up.

"What do you suppose he wants?" Mallory asked.

"I can't imagine," I said, and went on to fill her in on Uncle Harry.

As it turned out, Harry wasn't alone. He was followed in by a dour, muscular person roughly my age, whom he introduced simply as Clay. Clay nodded, then took in the surroundings with the detached manner of a bodyguard checking for sniper nests.

Uncle Harry ignored the room entirely. Even before an introduction could be made, he had sized up Mallory and decided how she would be played: not as a nonentity (as he might have done if it suited his purpose), but as a welcome addition to the Tull inner circle. This meant he judged she could be used as an ally in whatever venture he was engaged in here.

"Nice place," he said, finally pretending to be interested in our suite. "Haven't visited the Escorial in ages. What's that you're having?"

I poured two more brandies and invited them to sit down.

I couldn't remember a time when I'd seen Uncle Harry outside the environment of the Tull citadel. What struck me was that he seemed as much at home here as he did there. He'd walked into our suite and effortlessly made it his own.

He was briskly interrogating Mallory about her background and history, and she was as briskly feeding him whatever lies came to hand. Suddenly realizing that she was twitting him, he roared with laughter and gave me a wink as if congratulating me on having acquired a nimble-witted girl instead of a dunce.

It was an odd scene, made sinister by the very geniality of Harry's performance. Mallory seemed less intimidated than I was, behaving as if men like Harry were an old story to her. I found myself becoming rather irritated with them both. Presumably Harry was there to talk to *me*, so why the devil wasn't he getting on with it?

"So," he said after a bit, "how did you two meet?"

"We met at a gallery showing of my work," Mallory said.

"I see. So you're what—a painter?"

"That's right."

"Interesting," he said, glancing at me. "I somehow formed the impression you had something to do with Jason's work with the Resurrection Institute."

"The what?"

Now he seemed to have hit on the idea of playing the fool.

"Harry means the Reincarnation Institute," I explained.

"Actually, that's the case," Mallory said cheerfully. "I'm the reincarnation of a black whore who was hunted down and murdered in this city a few years after the glorious triumph at Dachau."

It was the first time I'd ever seen Uncle Harry take a hit from anybody. Shaken, he visibly searched for a chuckle but couldn't seem to find one anywhere.

"Jason," Mallory said, "Harry's glass is empty."

And so it was. So were most of them, in fact, except for Clay's, who was dutifully abstaining. I filled glasses, taking my time.

Harry settled back in his chair and crossed his legs, as if in preparation for a long stay. "I'm always glad to learn," he said after taking a sip of brandy. By now once again in command of himself, he gave Mallory an appreciative nod. "You've taught me something, and very economically too."

Mallory nodded back coolly.

"This young woman knows who she is," he said, turning to me.

"Mmmm," I said in agreement.

"Do you know who *you* are?"

Unprepared for such a question, I answered rather lamely. "I think so."

"I think *not*," he said.

"Excuse me, Uncle Harry," I said, wrapping myself in as much dignity as I could assemble about myself, "but it's getting late. Would you mind explaining why you're here?"

"I'm here to find out if you know who you are."

I shook my head in frustration.

"You think I'm trying to embarrass you in front of your girl," Harry said, reading my mind with total accuracy, "but in fact I'm here to spare you embarrassment."

"Explain how that works, Uncle Harry," I replied bitterly.

"I've known you since you were a toddler, Jason. And ever since I've known you, I've known that your greatest problem in life would be discovering who you are. This isn't something unique to you. The sons of men like Jason Tull always have difficulty discovering who they are—aside from being the junior version of their fathers. I'm sure you know exactly what I'm talking about, Jason. Being the junior version gets you the headwaiter's attention. It gets you a pair of seats at the opera when there are no seats. It gets you a respectful warning instead of a speeding ticket. You like getting all those things, but you know you don't get them because of who you are but because of who your father is. Being the junior version lets you move around like a prince, but it never lets you find out who you are in yourself. This is very much behind your interest in reincarnation, you know."

"Is it, now! What makes you think so?"

"Isn't it obvious? All the tales of reincarnation you've told us over the years are about people who have found out *who they are*—something you'd very much like to do for yourself. They're all your proxies in discovery. Like them, you'd love to wake up one morning and be someone else entirely. If you were no longer just a junior version of Jason Tull, then of course you'd *have* to know who you are."

"There's something in what you say, Harry—God knows there is—but I don't see why it's something that needs to be discussed on this particular night."

Harry looked at Mallory, who held his gaze for a moment then looked away. Turning back to me, he said, "This particular night is precisely when it needs to be discussed."

"Why?"

"If you had a better idea of who you are, then you'd know why."

"That's very clever, Harry, but I don't think it's more than that."

Again he looked at Mallory, as if expecting some kind of support from her. Again she looked away, but I could see she had something on her mind. Finally she gave me her eyes and said, "Jason, I think you've got to try and put this together."

"What do you mean?"

"Why is Harry here *tonight*?"

I looked at Harry, and he looked back, with suddenly ferocious intensity. "Who *are* you?" he said, as if genuinely in the dark and genuinely curious.

"Christ," I said, actually a little scared, "I don't know what the hell you're getting at."

"Who *are* you?" he insisted.

Feeling trapped, I staggered to my feet. "What the hell is he talking about, Mallory? Do you know?"

"I think he's trying to make you see why he's here *tonight*, Jason."

"Why *is* he here tonight?"

The two of them exchanged another glance.

"Harry's telling the truth, Jason. He's here tonight because you don't know who you are."

"This is bullshit," I said, meaning approximately, "Why are you two ganging up on me?"

Clay chose this moment to excuse himself, mumbling something about finding a bathroom.

I stood there glaring from Harry to Mallory and back again. Suddenly I felt *they* were the strangers, and it was I who should be asking *who are you?*

"What's going on here? What do you want from me?"

Turning to Mallory, Harry said, "I think Jason would rather hear this from you than from me."

"Sit down, Jason, please." I sat down. "I noticed this myself earlier, but I didn't think it was any of my business. It didn't even occur to me to mention it."

"Mention what?"

"That you're acting as if you don't exist. You spent the whole day doing it."

"I haven't the slightest idea what you're talking about."

"You're acting as if you were a piece of clear glass that everyone just looks straight through. You're acting as if you're invisible—as if you don't exist. And this is why Harry's here tonight. I saw it as soon as he started asking, 'Who are you?'"

"I wish *I* saw it. When was I acting like this?"

She sent a doubtful look Harry's way.

"Jason," he said, taking up the refrain, "the first person to whom you must become visible is you. You can't guide yourself using Mallory's eyes or my eyes. You have to see for yourself where you are. It does no good to use another's vision for this purpose."

"Riddles," I said, without conviction.

Clay chose that moment to return, letting the boss know with a nod that he was ready to resume his duties. Harry rose and reached for his topcoat, which had been slung over the back of a sofa.

"You're *leaving*?" I'm not sure which feeling was more predominant in me, relief or frustration.

"We're leaving, yes," Uncle Harry agreed.

"So nice of you to drop by," I told him, "though it isn't for me to say, strictly speaking."

He replied with a small, troubled shake of the head. Then he turned to Mallory and took her hand gravely for a moment before departing.

I didn't know what to make of or do about the awkwardness that was now loomingly in place between Mallory and me. I didn't want to go home in a huff, though it was certainly an option. The light touch seemed a better one, if I could manage it.

"Personally," I said, pouring us another pair of drinks, "I think we had a better time on the ladder."

She smiled, valiantly but not wholeheartedly.

I could think of several things I would've liked to hear her say, but none of them seemed to occur to her. She was stuck for a solid two minutes.

Then she said, "Let's not talk."

I hadn't thought of that one.

I woke at three in the morning, as I sometimes do, too full of ideas and plans to sleep. Reading for a while usually helps, so I pawed around for the books I'd parked on the night table on returning from Dial's bookstore. The Stein book was there but not the other two. Thinking they might have been knocked off onto the floor, I slid out of bed and checked. They weren't on the floor.

"What is it?" Mallory asked, turning over sleepily.

"Two of the books I bought today are gone."

Sitting up, she asked, "How could they be?"

"I don't know, but they're not here."

"Could you have taken them into the living room?"

"I could have, but I didn't."

"Why don't you check, just to be sure."

I checked. On returning, I said, "Harry's adjutant took them. That was what he did when he excused himself to go to the bathroom."

I could see that she'd already come to the same conclusion.

"Why did he do that?" I asked. "What's the point?"

"I don't know," she muttered, hardly above a whisper.

I stood there frowning down at her, feeling for the first time ever that she was lying to me. Maybe she didn't literally *know*, but she had a guess, and she wasn't sharing it with me.

"Both books can be replaced," I went on, "so what's the use of taking them?"

This time she said nothing.

"Give me a hint."

After thinking a while, she said, "You don't *take* hints, Jason. I've never known anyone worse at taking hints."

"Why did he take two and not all three?"

Mallory gazed up at me steadily without answering.

2 6

THE NEXT MORNING I was approaching the entrance to the Times Building when I heard my name called. It was Clay, by golly—Uncle Harry's attaché—standing by the open door of a black limousine.

"Dr. Whitaker would like a word with you," he said as I approached.

I started to get in, then backed out when I saw that Harry wasn't inside. "I've got an appointment here," I explained.

"It's all right," he told me. "You won't be late."

"I don't see how that's possible," I said, after checking my watch. "Can Dr. Whitaker stop time?"

"Dr. Whitaker can do most anything," Clay said with the ghost of a smile. Then, as he saw me hesitating, he added, "It's important."

He followed me in, and the driver pulled away from the curb.

"Would you mind taking off your jacket?" Clay asked. Since the temperature was in the sixties, I hadn't bothered with a topcoat.

"Why should I do that?"

"Because I have to give you a shot." He produced a leather case, which he unzipped to reveal two vials and a hypodermic syringe.

"What the hell is that?"

"What did I just say, Mr. Tull? I have to give you a shot."

"A shot of what?"

Clay sighed. "Dr. Whitaker said you'd probably ask that. Here's what he told me to tell you: 'This will make you visible.'"

"Bullshit."

"Yeah, well, he said you'd probably say that too."

We inched our way through three or four stoplights.

"The way I understand it," Clay said at last, "Dr. Whitaker is an old friend of the Tull family."

"That's right."

"But you think he might do you an injury. Is that right?"

"Not exactly."

Clay laughed. "You know, I didn't get all that stuff he was saying last night about you not knowing who you are. But I'm beginning to."

"How wonderful for you."

"I tell you what." He reached into a back pocket and pulled out a billfold. After examining the contents, he looked up at me and said, "In this job, I have to carry a lot of cash—or what's a lot of cash for me." He counted out four hundreds, eight fifties, and eight twenties, and put them on the seat between us. "I'll bet you this thousand—which I'll have to replace out of my own pocket if I lose it—that within five minutes of having this shot, you'll know who you are."

"What's in the syringe, some kind of psychotropic?"

He laughed again. "You really are a scream, Mr. Tull. Next you'll be asking if I'm going to put you into a trance."

I got out my own billfold and counted out seven hundreds and six fifties.

"Take off your jacket and roll up a sleeve."

He carefully swabbed a spot with alcohol from one of the two vials, then filled the syringe from the other. After administering the shot, he taped a bit of cotton over the puncture and helped me don my jacket again.

Then, having repacked the case, he sat back, looked at me with a pleasant smile, and said, "I see you, Mr. Tull."

I knew he did. By then—after a mere thirty seconds—the revelation was mostly complete, having no connection to whatever drug I'd been injected with. It had all come clear as the steel slid into my vein. It was as though the needle had been the conduit for enlightenment rather than some clear liquid.

As I'd dressed to go out an hour before, Mallory had asked where I was going. When I didn't answer immediately, she said, "Never mind. Forgive me for asking. It slipped my mind that you're the invisible man."

Now at last I got it.

I'd thought I could visit Dial's bookstore and be invisible. I'd thought I could make a very peculiar purchase there and no one would remark on it. I'd thought I could have a portentous conversation with a news editor at a globally influential paper and our words would vanish into the ether. I'd thought I could promise a sensational story and beg for an opportunity to discuss it, and no one would take notice of this or think it worth analyzing as an interesting event in its own right.

I had acted as if Edmund Dial would think of my visit this way: "When I walked into my office, I expected to see Jason Tull, but it wasn't Jason Tull after all, it was someone else."

I carried and gave out personal cards all the time. Naturally they said, "Jason Tull, Jr." What they should have said was, "NOT Jason Tull." Because I was NOT Jason Tull, it somehow followed that I was invisible. I could go anywhere and do anything without being noticed. People looked through me as if I were a sheet of clear glass.

I knew only who I was *not*.

This was what Uncle Harry intended to demonstrate by having Clay lift the two books from my bedside table: *Behold! You are SEEN. You are NOT invisible. Behold! I've come here this evening to purloin two books out of the three that you are KNOWN to have purchased. I even know which two I want to take in order to demonstrate your visibility.*

As this went through my head, I didn't take note of the fact that I was fading out, disappearing into a sort of vast mind-numbing cloud.

The last thing I clearly remember was shoving my thousand dollars across the seat into Clay's hand.

2 7

I WOKE DYING, or at least wishing I was dead, on a cot in a tiny room with a boarded window. My throat was raw, and judging from the taste in my mouth, this was the result of throwing up everything inside of me. My head was pounding in a way that carried pain outward to the very surface of my throbbing skin and eyeballs. I wanted water, but I wanted to relapse into unconsciousness even more.

I turned over, away from the wall, prayerfully imagining that some saintly person might have left a bottle of water within reach, and there, by God, it was—a quart. I fished it up from the floor, opened it, finished off half of it in one swallow, and plunged back into unconsciousness.

I woke again in another four hours or twelve hours. There was enough light seeping through the window to convince me it was day. The blessed bottle was there on the floor at my bedside, and I finished it off in another long gulp. My headache was only a memory, but it was still a potent one. I wasn't ready for three sets of tennis, but I was ready to get out of that room. At least I wasn't a prisoner. The door to the room stood open, revealing a hall outside.

Not more than five minutes were needed to explore the entire building, which appeared to have served at one time as a military or scientific installation, permanently manned by two or three people but occasionally visited (I surmised) by another dozen, who used a sort of office or classroom at the front. Of more immediate significance to me was the fact that the building stood in the center of a vast, featureless wasteland that have might have been the moon if it weren't for the scruffy vegetation that extended on all sides to the horizon. There were the remains of automotive ruts leading to the west (as I judged it to be, since the sun was steadily rising in the other direction), but there were no fresh tire tracks to be seen. Incredibly, it appeared that I'd been airlifted in.

Once it was established that I wasn't going to leave on foot, I went back inside to consider the setup of the briefing room at the front of the building. At the back of this room was a low platform with a swivel chair positioned on it. The chair, unlike the other furniture in the room, was clean and new—an obvious import. A freshly cleaned chalkboard was mounted on the wall behind the chair, and several objects were arranged to face it: two floodlights, a video camera, and a television set, all connected to massive commercial batteries. Sitting down in the chair, I saw that the camera and the television set were both turned on.

The screen showed a scene that was almost a mirror

image of the one I was standing in, with an empty desk and an empty chair behind it. I sat down and fixed my eyes on the screen, waiting for something to happen.

Nothing happened.

Obviously something was *going* to happen. Why else assemble all this equipment here and all that equipment there (wherever "there" was)?

I waited. I watched.

I said to myself, *obviously they didn't expect me to recover consciousness this soon* (whoever "they" were).

I still had my watch (along with everything else). It said it was eleven, manifestly in the morning, though I rather doubted I was still in the Eastern time zone.

I went on sitting there, waiting, watching. Nothing went on happening.

At noon, all the water I'd taken in had filtered down to my bladder, and I went outside to get rid of it. While I was there, I took the time to survey again the bleak desert surrounding me. At the end of the rutted road, which disappeared in the haze at the horizon, no cloud of dust was being raised by an approaching vehicle. No helicopters were clattering their way to me.

I went back inside, sat down at the desk, and watched the screen, as empty-headed as a lizard on a rock. I was like someone in a movie theater waiting for the lights to go down and the show to start. The only things going through my mind were equivalent to *Where is it?* and *What's the holdup?*

On the screen in front of me absolutely nothing was happening. There wasn't even a clock ticking off the seconds on the wall behind the empty chair.

At two o'clock I could no longer ignore the fact that I was

ravenously hungry. Surely whoever had deposited me here had left some food to go with the water. I wasn't intended to perish, after all . . . surely. There would be a box somewhere, with something edible in it, even if it was only candy bars and crackers. Fruit, maybe, or even something tinned. I could picture it as clearly as if I'd already seen it—a corrugated cardboard box, kraft brown. It would be really terrible, I thought, if they'd forgotten to include a can opener. Such things happen.

But of course there was no box. There was a kitchen of sorts, still furnished with heavy dishes and a few battered pots and pans, but bare of food, except, absurdly, for a box of rice, hard as a brick and with the dust of decades on it. Predictably, nothing came from the tap in the sink.

I went back to my vigil in front of the television screen.

By five o'clock I realized I was beginning to lose control, partly because five o'clock is "quitting time," when whoever was supposed to be sitting in that chair on the screen would be knocking off work to go home to dinner.

Who did these people think they were dealing with? Some nobody?

I went on watching for another two hours because there was absolutely nothing else to do.

At seven, when I took another bathroom break outside, the sun was still high in the sky, confirming my notion that I was a lot closer to the Pacific coast than to the Atlantic. I eyed the road, wondering what was at the end of it. If, as I'd always been assured, the horizon was twenty miles away, then it would, I estimated, take me five hours of walking to reach the vacancy that was presently visible to me—with no guarantee that anything besides more vacancy would be visible from that vantage point. And even if something besides vacancy *was* visible, would I be able to cross this desert without a drop of water?

The thought of water sent me back inside to see if the bottle I'd sucked dry in the morning really was completely dry. Except for about three drops I was able to coax from the bottom, it was. But in desperation I got down on my stomach to check under the cot and found a treasure: another quart bottle, half full, that I'd evidently gulped at before I was entirely conscious. The cap was only lightly screwed down, and I gave it another hasty twist, as if the half-quart were going to evaporate before my very eyes.

I've heard or read somewhere that the thing to do in this situation is to drink down your water reserves straightaway. However logically or physiologically correct this advice may be, whoever formulated it is a damned fool. There was no way in the world I was going to empty that bottle, no matter how much I longed to.

I took a quick sip and screwed the cap down hard.

Then, feeling decidedly heartened (and having nothing better to do), I went back to my watching post. Nothing had changed. The room on the screen remained brightly lit and utterly empty.

In two hours, I said to myself, *I'll have another sip*, and set the bottle down firmly in the center of the desk, so that even if some malign force were to tip it over, no harm would come to it.

Night fell, eventually. I considered turning on the battery-powered lights that were trained on me but shrugged the idea off. What was there to see, after all?

In the dark, facing only the lighted television screen, I

realized belatedly what point Uncle Harry was making with it (for I had no doubt whatever that he was behind all this). I, seated in a chair behind a desk, was looking at another chair behind another desk. Harry was holding up a mirror for me to look into, and, looking into this mirror, I was seeing myself, seeing what someone would see looking into the room in which I sat: a vacant chair. Or, alternatively, an invisible man.

There was certainly no argument about that. I'd been living for a long, long time as an invisible man. In a sense, my work for the Fenshaws was designed to reduce my invisibility, for certainly *they* saw me. They didn't know my father from Adam. They knew *me*, and me alone.

But who exactly was that?

What would they say if someone asked them who I was?

"Oh . . . Jason? Terribly nice chap. Earnest, intelligent, conscientious, well-educated. Perfect manners, delightful sense of humor—not pretentious at all, though he's supposedly very well connected, important family, all that." Could they conceivably say more than this?

I thought about the people closest to me. My father was Somebody, no doubt about that. My mother was Somebody. Uncle Harry. Both the Fenshaws. Mallory, even in a state of deep psychological shock, was Somebody.

How exactly had this result come about?

My father, Harry, the Fenshaws, and Mallory were driven . . . by ambition, goals, dreams. Certainly that was part of it—but not all of it, since Mother wasn't in the least driven, by anything. If the Tull fortune were to melt away overnight, she would be less devastated than my father. She would shrug and carry on exactly as before, except without the wherewithal to maintain a baronial lifestyle. She was self-possessed. She possessed herself and needed no more, though she certainly knew how to use more if there *was* more.

Had I missed a course in school—*How To Be a Person*?

Was the key that they all *cared deeply* about something? It was certainly true that each had a center around which his or her life revolved. But what was mine? Did I deeply care whether I actually someday made a Golden Case for the Fenshaws? Not really, I had to admit. Would making it fill (to even a slight extent) the yawning vacancy within Jason Tull, Jr.? This seemed doubtful. But what would fill it? What in fact *did* I care about?

Even at the time, I didn't imagine that these were profound thoughts I was having. They seemed more like the thoughts of a schoolboy who has failed to get a date for the prom, and the only profound effect they had was to make me long for sleep.

When I dragged myself into the briefing room the next morning, I headed straight for the bottle of water, which I had thought prudent to leave sitting on the desk. Only after taking a swig did I notice that a change had taken place in the scene on the television screen. A man was sitting behind the desk reading a book. When I sat down, he looked up, set the book aside, and said, "Good morning, Jason."

It took me a moment to register that it was Ward Woolton, my acquaintance on the *New York Times*. He'd gained some weight since college days, filling out what had already been a nearly square face, and his dark hair had receded a bit to enhance the effect.

"What's going on here?" I demanded.

"You'll find a clip-on microphone there on the chair, I believe, and I'm told there are some floodlights. Are they turned on?" When I'd attached the microphone to the placket of my shirt and switched on the floodlights, he said that was better, and I repeated my query.

"That's a large question, Jason," Ward replied. "Among other things that are going on here, the moon is circling the earth, the earth is circling the sun, and the sun is circling whatever it circles."

"I want to know what I'm doing here."

"Let's try and get things straight at the outset, Jason. I have no idea where you are or what you're doing there. All I know is that I'm sitting here watching a televised picture of you, and you're sitting there watching a televised picture of me. I'm in New York City. Where you are is unknown to me, as is the purpose for your being there."

"You've got to know more than that. Why are you sitting there?"

"I'm sitting here because I was told to sit here."

"You work for Harry Whitaker?"

"Who the hell is Harry Whitaker? Or do you mean the Intelligence wallah?"

"That's who I mean."

Ward chuckled. "My wife'll get a kick out of that. No, I don't work for Harry Whitaker. I work for my boss, who works for his boss, who works for his boss, who for all I know has lunch with Harry Whitaker on alternate Tuesdays at the Yale Club."

"What are you supposed to do sitting there?"

"I'm supposed to talk to you till you write three words on the chalkboard behind you."

"What three words?"

"Dear boy," Ward said, "try not to be a complete ass. If I knew the three magic words, I'd tell you straightaway and go to lunch."

"How will you know if the three I write are the right ones?"

"Ah," he said, beaming with pleasure. "I have a cunning little gizmo here at my right hand with a button and two lights, one red and one green. When I press the button, someone in another room checks his screen to see what you've written and then signals green for yes or red for no."

"What happens when I finally get it right?"

"I haven't a clue."

I got up, found the chalk that had been provided, and wrote I Am Visible on the board. Ward pressed the button on his gizmo, and a moment later his phone rang. He answered, listened, and informed me that my lettering had been judged insufficiently legible. I needed to make it heavier. After I did so, Ward watched his gizmo complacently, then reported a no.

"Evidently," he said, "your visibility or lack of same is not of interest."

"How do I know if I come close but miss by one word or something?"

"I guess you don't."

"I'd like something to eat."

"I'm told they'll be sending in a sandwich for me around noon, if it takes that long. Perhaps they're planning to do the same for you."

"Don't be ridiculous."

He shrugged. "I know nothing about your situation, so I don't know what's ridiculous and what isn't."

"I need some more water."

"Then go get some."

"There isn't any here. There was some, but this is all that's left of it." I held up the bottle, now four-fifths empty. Ward shrugged. "Call and tell them I need more water."

"I'm sorry, but that isn't the setup here. They can call me but I can't call them. All I can do is push the button on the gizmo."

I got up and wrote I NEED WATER on the board. Ward pressed his button, watched his gizmo, then shook his head. "Sorry," he said, "not the magic words."

"They weren't meant to be the magic words. They were meant to be a communication."

"Maybe they're not wired for sound and just get the picture. That's all they care about, after all—the three words."

I tried SEND IN HARRY.

No.

"Look, old man, maybe you should just get down to it instead of fucking about like this."

"What do you mean by 'get down to it'?"

Ward made a face. "Jason, when we were at school together, it often seemed to me that teachers gave you more credit than you deserved. Nothing you've said or done today has changed that estimate."

"Go on."

"I have no idea why you're there—wherever 'there' is. Hasn't it occurred to you to wonder why *I'm* here? Why me in particular?"

Mallory had asked a very similar question two nights before: "Why is Harry here *tonight*?" I was beginning to wonder if the way I was feeling is how people feel after a lobotomy.

"You're there," I said, "because I called and made an appointment to see you."

"Bravo, Jason. You called and made an appointment to see me about . . . ?"

"About a story."

"Bravo again, Jason. I regard this as a *strong* clue." He spoke with heavy irony, as well he might.

"So, in effect, they want me to keep my appointment with you, and this will ultimately lead me to produce three words they have in mind."

"That's certainly how it looks, old man. Why don't you start by telling me what you planned to tell me twenty-four hours ago?"

"I'd rather just produce the three words and go home."

"By all means. Go to it. Fire away."

I lost faith in what I was writing halfway through, but went ahead anyway: IT DOESN'T MATTER. I wasn't even sure what the statement was supposed to mean, now that it was up there. I rubbed it out and sat down again to gather my thoughts.

"The five-minute limit is meaningless now," I said at last.

"What five-minute limit do you mean?"

"You said you'd give me five minutes to explain my story."

Ward chuckled. "Mere journalistic bluster, old boy. I wanted you to focus your thoughts before you arrived rather than while sitting at my desk."

"I'm afraid it didn't do much good. I've no idea how to begin."

"Give me the lead. That's always a good place to start."

"What's a lead?"

"Here's a lead. 'The parents of Hansel and Gretel were arrested for child endangerment this morning, according to police sources within the Great Forest.'"

"I don't think I can do it that way. The Grimms didn't either."

"Don't give up on it yet, Jason. The lead just takes the who, what, when, and where of a story and puts them all together in one sentence. If you've got a story, it's certainly about someone, and this someone must've done something or had something done to him, and this must've happened at some particular time and place."

"That's all true of this story."

"Splendid. So start with the who. Who are the who of your story?"

"*We* are the who."

"You mean the Tulls?"

"No, not the Tulls."

"Who then? The people of New York City? The people of America? What?"

"All of us."

"You mean the whole human race?"

"No. The *Aryan* race."

He looked puzzled. "The Aryan race is what the human

race has *become*, Jason. Just as *Homo sapiens sapiens* is what the human race has become."

I had at that moment a flash of inspiration that lifted the hair on the back of my neck. "Here's my lead, Ward. 'The Aryan race was today charged with making itself the human race by murdering all other member races of *Homo sapiens sapiens* during the early centuries of the present era.'"

His look of puzzlement dissolved into open astonishment. "That's not half bad, Jason," he said, evidently impressed not so much by the content of what I'd said as by the fact that I'd said it. "But how does the story go from there? You say the Aryan race was 'today charged'—by whom? In what court?"

"I guess I have to say by me, in the court of public opinion."

"Hmmm. On whose authority do you make the charge? What weight does a charge by you carry? As far as I know, you're just a private citizen."

"That's true."

"And the court of public opinion meets very irregularly, to say the least. All the same. . ." He paused to think. "What evidence are you bringing forward to support the charge?"

"The evidence of our children's textbooks, going back a thousand years."

"Interesting."

At that moment he was interrupted by the arrival of someone in the room from which he was broadcasting. "Excuse me," he said. "It's my lunch. Would you rather I took it somewhere else?"

"No, go ahead and eat. Just try not to enjoy it too much."

He nodded just as if I'd said something to be taken seriously, then waded into his sandwich. "In effect," he said, after swallowing a bite, "you're just offering a new interpretation of what's in those textbooks."

I thought about that some. "At their arraignment, Hansel and Gretel's parents said, 'In effect you're just offering a new interpretation of our actions. From our point of view, we were only doing the best we could for the tykes. Ma and I were broke and starving, so we thought the kids could do better on their own. We never wanted anything but the best for them.'"

Ward was nodding enthusiastically. "Okay, that's damned good—so long as it's just between you and me. But I'm afraid it's not going to play very well for a wider audience. Hansel and Gretel's parents are one thing. Fifty generations of journalists, dramatists, novelists, screenwriters, historians, curriculum writers, and schoolteachers are another. Surely you can see that."

"I can see it. All the same, the facts are not in question."

"Perfectly correct," said Ward. "Hansel and Gretel were ditched in the forest by their parents."

"And we systematically purged the world of every race but our own."

Ward took a bite of his sandwich and gazed into the eye of the camera. When he finished chewing, he said, "Where do we go from there?"

I got up and wrote three words on the chalkboard: WE'RE ALL MURDERERS.

He shrugged and jabbed the button on his gizmo. "Sorry," he said after a moment. "Those three don't do anything for them—or for me, to be honest. Maybe you should think about what you want to accomplish with the story. What are you hoping for—waves of mass suicidal remorse?"

"No."

"Then what's the point of issuing a statement like 'We're all murderers'?"

"Forget it. I'm grasping at straws. I'm thirsty."

The swine chose that moment to take a long swallow of beer. He patted his lips with a napkin, then asked again what I wanted to accomplish.

"I want to wake people up to the pious lies they learned in school."

"And those are. . . ?"

"That we were acting for the good of humanity when we exterminated the native peoples of Asia, Africa, and the New World. That we murdered billions of people out of sheer selfless nobility."

Ward nodded thoughtfully. "I guess that is the way it's taught. But I'm not sure it isn't taken with a grain of salt."

"Did *you* take it with a grain of salt?"

"I took *everything* with a grain of salt."

"So this was nothing special."

"No, not really. It was just one more piece of ancient history, like the sack of Rome or the Norman Conquest— nothing to do with me."

"Has this conversation changed the way you feel about it?"

"Truthfully, not even by a hair."

"It doesn't trouble you that the systematic extermination of all these people is represented as a sort of sacred undertaking?"

"How would you like it to be represented?"

"As a ghastly crime—the most terrible in human history—committed by our immediate ancestors."

"All the crimes of history were committed by our ancestors—every single one of them—every murder, rape, assault, assassination, and enslavement. Who else would have committed them if not our ancestors?"

"But this crime was committed by the people who turned the entire human race into *us*. It was committed by the people who secured the earth for the Aryan race alone."

Ward shrugged and shook his head.

"This doesn't move you," I persisted.

"Move me to what? Tears? Remorse? Indignation? I'm afraid not, honestly."

"All right. Tell me this. Are you speaking personally now or as an editor?"

"How do you perceive the difference?"

"As an editor, you must assign a lot of stories that don't have any relevance or fascination to you personally."

"Very true."

"As an editor, you can't select only the ones you'd personally like to see. You're selecting stories for the entire readership of your newspaper."

"Absolutely."

"So which judgment are you giving me here? Your personal judgment or your professional judgment?"

"I'm giving you both. They're not always in conflict, after all. In this case, your story's a nonstarter, for me and for the readership of the *Times*."

"Amazing," I said. "It's so simple. How could I have missed it?"

"What do you mean?"

I got up and chalked in three new words.

"You've got something there," Mark said. "Even if it's no more than what I've been telling you for the last ten minutes. All the same, these may not be the magic words."

"Press the button, Mark."

He did so and a moment later turned to me with a raffish grin.

"You're right at last, Jason. *No one cares.* I think you can count on that."

He drained his glass, wiped his lips, and said, "So how is your mother, Jason? You know, I met her once. An amazing woman."

The helicopter arrived an hour later.

EPILOGUE

People can simply never get used to everything that a corpse can do.

28

TWO MONTHS AND ten days later, the following story appeared in the *New York Daily Globe*.

"Croatan" Gallery as Baffling as Its Ancient Namesake

Normally unflappable New Yorkers were audibly and visibly flapped at the black-tie, invitation-only grand opening of a bizarre gallery-bookstore that is the brainchild of dark-horse socialite Jason Tull, Jr.

On Friday night, more than 200 guests from the city's beau monde gathered at the Croatan gallery on Broadway at Madison Square to examine a collection of art and literature allegedly unseen in 2000 years.

It was the opinion of more than one visitor that the collection should remain unseen for another 2000.

Especially featured was an exhibit of the work of Negro photographer Roy DeCarava, a collection of dark and often enigmatic images of New York City in the decade or so following the victory at Dachau. Many of his pictures invite the philistine to wonder why they were taken in the first place. One must spend a few minutes in intimate communion with a picture like "Girl Looking Back" before its mysterious gravitic attraction begins to take effect, but "Two Women with Mannequin's Hand" remained mute for me no matter how often I returned to it. "Couple at the Museum of Modern Art" was amusingly relevant in this setting, since the couple in question are planted in front of three examples of exactly the sort of art Croatan supposedly exists to rescue from oblivion—ugly smudges that might have come up directly from a heavily traveled industrial roadway.

Less appealing than DeCarava's work were lithographs from four other artists of the period, all typical of the degenerate styles nurtured by the Jewish dealers and critics who so decisively shaped the "modern art" phenomenon. Three paintings in the same vein from a contemporary artist, Mallory Hastings, are also on view. According to the painter (who is coincidentally affianced to gallery-owner Tull), these three large works represent a style known briefly in the postwar years as "abstract expressionism." Very expressive and very abstract, they invite the philistine to wonder if his four-year-old could do as well, given a sufficient supply of fingerpaints.

Owner Tull explains both the name and the concept of the gallery this way. At the end of the 17th century 100 of the earliest English settlers in the New World came to be known as "the Lost Colony" when they inexplicably vanished from Roanoke Island, leaving behind a single enigmatic trace: the word "Croatan," carved in a tree trunk.

Since the artists Tull intends to showcase constitute a similarly "lost" colony composed of many mongrel races, now long extinct, the name Croatan recommended itself as an appropriate evocation of their forgotten existence.

Tull has taken the trouble to republish several literary and scientific works from the Lost Colony. One of the volumes on display is *The Interpretation of Dreams* by a Viennese Jew alleged to have influenced the thinking of depth psychologist C.G. Jung. Another is *Relativity: The Special and the General Theory* by a German Jew similarly alleged to have anticipated some of the central ideas of particle physics. Several purely literary works include volumes from authors with names like Stein, Kafka, Zangwill, and Büchner

It was not a long night as such nights go. Many guests entered, spun about on a heel, and departed without even touching a ritual glass of champagne. Out of earshot of the Tull family circle, one heard comments like "waste of time," "insulting," and "appalling." There were also comments like "interesting," "different," and "provocative," though to be fair these were heard mostly within earshot of the Tull family circle, which by nine o'clock seemed to be running out of smiles. By nine-thirty smiles no longer mattered, since there was no longer anyone around to see them.

All the same, Croatan is well worth a visit, for it represents a curious and rather ghastly monument, rather like an ancient, bloodstained pyramid emerging from a jungle. Like many monuments of that kind, it both impresses and bewilders . . . inviting even the most kindly disposed philistine to wonder if perhaps young Jason Tull isn't engaged in an elaborate leg-pull and snickering at us all from behind his hand.

• • •

This was a rather middle-of-the-road account of the opening, which would have been widely covered even without the efforts of the family publicist.

Reactions to the gallery within the family were entirely predictable. Mother thought the whole project was original, valiant, and fascinating. Father did a first-class job of pretending that he wasn't embarrassed and didn't think the whole thing a colossal waste of time, talent, and money.

Mallory warned me before the opening that each of the attending critics would seek out one item to praise warmly and another to praise reservedly, and then, having manifested all this open-mindedness and fair-handedness, would maul the rest of the show with an easy conscience.

Surprisingly, three of DeCarava's photos sold at the opening. Except for the republished books, nothing else was for sale. In all, seven books left the shop; I later checked the trash basket at the corner and found that three of them hadn't made it any farther than that. Mallory declined to put prices on her paintings, pointing out that if none were for sale, none could fail to sell.

Business aside, the opening had some aspects of an Old Home Week event. Mr. and Mrs. Hastings, Mallory's "parents" (she always insists on the quote marks), made a brief, noisy appearance, looking as uneasy as two parrots on display at a cat show. The Fenshaws were there (I'd sent them plane tickets), Reggie in evening wear so dashingly antique that it looked positively Edwardian and Marcia in a dreadful thrift-shop gown in which she obviously felt very glamorous. They tried hard to persuade Mallory that she "owed it to the world" to give them a firsthand account of her experience for their newsletter. They tried hard to persuade me that I would soon be ready for new investigative assignments, and looked positively crestfallen when I handed them a check that would keep We Live Again going for another five years, for they knew this meant I'd never be coming back to Tunis.

To no one's surprise, Uncle Harry didn't show up at the opening. Not his style. He quaintly sent a telegram bearing his best wishes. He hadn't contacted me following my "lesson in the desert," and I hadn't expected him to. We understood each other. At last.

Croatan was an outgrowth of my comprehension and acceptance of the fact that "no one cared" about my great revelation. Croatan was what I would do *despite* the fact that no one cared. It was what I would do because *I* cared. None of that would have to be explained to Harry.

I did not, of course, become a shopkeeper when Croatan opened. That was never in my mind. I hired a young woman named Tanya, who had been an assistant manager at another gallery.

Quite a lot of money was spent on the design of the place. We wanted people to feel they could come in and browse without being expected to buy something. Croatan was to feel almost like an open arcade, an extension of the street, and it succeeded in this. Because of the gallery's publicity and its enticing entrance, we received a surprising amount of foot traffic. Not sales. We didn't expect sales, we hoped for interest, attention.

Then one night we got really lucky. Someone heaved a paving stone through the front window. We were ecstatic.

Someone *got it*. Someone *cared*.

I contacted our publicist early the following morning and directed her to alert all the news media to this event.

"This isn't the kind of publicity you want," she informed me.

"Oh, but it is, my dear. Don't quote me, of course, but it's very much the kind of publicity we want. Tell everyone that we'll be replacing the window with specially strengthened glass. This will give the next brick-heaver something to aspire to."

A few days later Uncle Harry dropped in and left his card. Tanya told me he'd spent almost an hour in the shop. He'd bought copies of the books by Freud and Einstein, as well as my favorite of the DeCarava photographs, of a tense and wary-looking Aryan couple on Fifth Avenue. He asked if I ever came to the shop, and she informed him I was there every Monday morning.

2 9

UNCLE HARRY STROLLED into the shop on the following Monday at eleven. I was glad to see he'd left Clay behind.

We greeted each other as if nothing like a hypodermic needle had ever come between us.

I said, "I assume you heard about our brick-thrower."

"Oh yes. Nice bit of luck for you."

"You don't seem upset to find out that *someone* cares, after all."

"Certainly not. One can't learn anything from being *right*, you know. How is Mallory liking it?"

"Liking what?"

"Her studio, the engagement, the gallery, her work."

"She seems generally pleased but feels she's leaving

abstract expressionism behind and moving on to something new."

"I thought she would."

"Doubtless so," I sneered, "having added art criticism to your many accomplishments."

He hadn't heard me. He went on to say, "I really admire that girl."

"I can tell you that you won't remain her favorite uncle if you continue to refer to her as 'that girl.'"

He smiled and shook his head indulgently. "I brought you this," he said, drawing a portfolio-size envelope from under his arm and handing it to me.

"What is it?"

"Since you've taken up publishing, I thought you might like producing something original for a change, instead of just reprinting old work."

At this point we took the conversation into a tiny office at the back, normally Tanya's hideout. When we were seated, I opened the envelope and drew out a plastic-wrapped package containing three school-type notebooks. As I started to unwrap them, Harry said, "Use them gently, Jason. They're two thousand years old and not made of the finest paper in the world."

I turned back the cover of the notebook on top to have a peek inside. "It looks like German."

"Not German," Harry said. "Something rarer, I'm told. Dutch."

"Where did they come from?"

"No one knows, really. They came to light rather like the last doll in a set of nesting dolls, found inside a pouch inside a box inside a file cabinet inside a Washington warehouse, to which the cabinet had been routed by mistake just after the war. There they sat, century after century, since the cabinet didn't belong to anyone and wasn't of interest to anyone. The pouch itself was date-stamped September 1944, with a handwritten message in German that said, 'See if the Commissioner wants these.'"

"Why do you think they deserve to be published?"

Harry shrugged. "I have no idea whether they deserve to be published or not, Jason. You're the publisher, not me. They were found entirely by accident and referred to me entirely by accident, and I had the choice of throwing them in the trash or bringing them to you. Publish them or pulp them—it makes no difference to me."

On his way out, Harry asked when Mallory and I intended to be married. I told him we were in no hurry and hadn't set a date.

"I would accept an invitation to dinner," he informed me solemnly.

"That's good to know, Uncle Harry. Mallory's a great admirer of yours, too, as you probably realize."

I made some enquiries and confirmed my guess, that Dutch had been extinct for a very, very long time—some seventeen or eighteen centuries, in fact. After more inquiries, I tracked down a scholar of ancient European languages and arranged to send her the notebooks for identification and evaluation.

After waiting several months I finally have her report and must decide whether to have the notebooks translated into

English or not. I must say I rather fancy the idea of becoming a real publisher and bringing out something never seen in print before in the whole history of the world.

I wonder what Mallory will think when I tell her my first offering as a publisher of original material will be the diary of another young woman who was hunted down for extermination, a Jewish teenager named Anne Frank.

A NOTE TO READERS

The story of Mary Anne Dorson was based loosely on that of Lurancy Vennum, born in Watseka, Illinois, in 1865. Lurancy's story was told in the local newspaper, in the pages of many spiritualist magazines, in the book *The Watseka Wonder* by E. W. Stevens (one of the physicians involved in the case), and in a modern retelling, *Watseka*, by David St. Clair, published in 1977 by Playboy Press but currently out of print.

Knowing how interested readers are in my beliefs, I should add that, although I employ fantastic elements in my novels when they serve my purpose, this shouldn't be taken as an assertion of their reality. For example, I have no personal belief in reincarnation or in the transmigration of souls, and it's no part of my intention in this book to promote these beliefs.

DANIEL QUINN